"I Will Not Be Insulted In My Own Cabin."

"Kindly leave."

"You don't mean that."

"I most certainly do! From the moment I came on deck this morning you treated me as though I were some kind of criminal."

"That's ridiculous! You're an intelligent woman. How do you manage to come up with such crackpot notions?"

"I am an intelligent woman! But you seem determined to treat me like a not very bright child."

"Oh, really? And I suppose last night I was treating you like a child?"

At the mention of the love they had shared, Cassia began to tremble. What an incredible difference a few hours could make!

MAURA SEGER

was prompted by a love of books and a vivid imagination to decide, at age twelve, to be a writer. Twenty years later, her first book was published. So much, she says, for overnight success! Now each book is an adventure, filled with fascinating people who always surprise her.

Dear Reader:

There is an electricity between two people in love that makes everything they do magic, larger than life. This is what we bring you in SILHOUETTE INTIMATE MOMENTS.

SILHOUETTE INTIMATE MOMENTS are longer, more sensuous romance novels filled with adventure, suspense, glamor or melodrama. These books have an element no one else has tapped: excitement.

We are proud to present the very best romance has to offer from the very best romance writers. In the coming months look for some of your favorite authors such as Elizabeth Lowell, Nora Roberts, Erin St. Claire and Brooke Hastings.

SILHOUETTE INTIMATE MOMENTS are for the woman who wants more than she has ever had before. These books are for you.

Karen Solem
Editor-in-Chief
Silhouette Books

Golden Chimera

Maura Seger

Silhouette Intimate Moments

Published by Silhouette Books New York

America's Publisher of Contemporary Romance

Silhouette Books by Maura Seger

A Gift Beyond Price (SE #135)
Silver Zephyr (IM #61)
Golden Chimera (IM #96)

SILHOUETTE BOOKS
300 E. 42nd St., New York, N.Y. 10017

Distributed by Pocket Books

ISBN: 0-373-07096-9

First Silhouette Books printing May, 1985

10 9 8 7 6 5 4 3 2 1

All of the characters in this book are fictitious. Any resemblance to actual persons, living or dead, is purely coincidental.

America's Publisher of Contemporary Romance

Printed in the U.S.A.

To Agatha, my Apple III.

Without her, none of this
would have been possible.

Golden Chimera

Chapter 1

"CASSIA," THE VOICE BESIDE THE BED INTONED QUIET-ly, "it's time to get up."

No response. The sleeping figure did not stir. Silver-blond hair spread out over the pillow framed a delicately featured face relaxed in repose. A thin sheet covering the slender form rose and fell with each measured breath.

"Cassia," the voice repeated more insistently, "you're due at Allegra and Simon's party in one hour."

Nothing. More dramatic measures were called for.

A red light blinked, there was a brief whirring sound, and the strains of a Vivaldi concerto filled the room.

"Mmmmm . . . W-what . . . ?" At last the figure moved reluctantly.

Translucent lids fluttered, opening to reveal blue-gray eyes. Cassia stared up at the ceiling for a moment, trying to recover from her too brief nap. Slowly her gaze shifted to the table beside the bed.

On the table was a box about fourteen inches long, eight inches deep, and eleven inches high. Its outer casing was of beige smudge-proof plastic. The front of it, facing Cassia, contained a small screen about eleven inches in diagonal, a blinking red light, and a speaker.

The box did not look all that different from any of the millions of small computers to be found in homes across the country. But there was one crucial difference.

Through it, Cassia was linked to the most advanced network of artificial intelligence in existence. A super-computer designed to mimic the most powerful thinking machine ever created, the human brain.

"Veda," Cassia asked groggily, "what time is it?"

"Seven P.M. Eastern Standard time," the computer answered promptly. "The temperature is sixty-five degrees Fahrenheit. There is a ten-mile-per-hour wind from the northwest. You should wear a coat."

The voice from the box was soft and melodious, pitched to a feminine frequency. That was only fitting, since Cassia had programmed more than a little of her own personality into the computer that was part essential tool, part mother hen.

"Thank you. I'd like some coffee."

A split second's hesitation before, "Have you read the latest report on the potential dangers of caffeine?"

In the midst of rising from the bed, Cassia frowned. She was supposed to know everything there was to know about the computer, yet sometimes Veda surprised her. Lately, she seemed to be taking an awful lot on herself.

Resisting the impulse to snap back, since that was patently silly with a machine, she said firmly, "Coffee, Veda. Now."

Was that a disparaging sniff she heard? Making a mental note to take another look at Veda's main circuit boards, Cassia headed for the shower.

Like the rest of the small but luxurious apartment at the Center for Advanced Research, the bathroom boasted the latest in microprocessor-driven technology. She had only to step over the threshold for the lights to come on and the ventilation fan to start up.

Slipping out of her nightgown, she said, "Shower."

The water in the cubicle came on instantly, at predetermined pressure and temperature levels. A slot precisely at hand level opened to dispense shampoo and soap.

As Cassia washed away the lingering traces of sleep, she thought about the party she was going to that evening. It would be good to see Simon and Allegra again. Their recent marriage was clearly a tremendous success; they radiated a sense of happiness that was as mysterious as it was enviable.

Seeing them together had made Cassia aware that there was a part of life she knew nothing about. Inevitably, her restless curiosity had led her to wonder about this strange thing called love.

She wasn't sure she had ever experienced it, even back when she was a child. Her family life, what little there had been of it, had ended when she was six years old.

Routine tests given when she entered the first grade had revealed a startlingly high level of intelligence. Psychologists and teachers alike had recommended that she receive special schooling to take full advantage of her potential.

For her parents, who had always been puzzled and even troubled by her, the news provided a welcome solution. They could do what the experts said was best for her and at the same time free themselves from the burden of a child who, unlike their other two, was not blessedly ordinary.

Tipping her head back to rinse away the shampoo, Cassia wondered absently if her parents were still living in Connecticut. The last time she had spoken with them, about four months before, they had mentioned they might be moving soon.

She felt no great sense of urgency to know where they were. Over the years, her contact with her family had dwindled down to no more than rare phone calls and impersonal presents exchanged at Christmas.

Cassia didn't really blame them for sending her away; she knew that in many ways she had benefited greatly. But without an outlet for her emotions, she had withdrawn even farther behind the wall of her differentness.

Only a very few people, most particularly Allegra and Simon, had ever managed to reach beyond that barrier. And even with them, the most Cassia could feel was friendship.

Mindful of the passing time, she finished rinsing her hair and said, "Dry." The water switched off, and was replaced by warm jets of air that moved gently over her body.

When the last droplets of water had evaporated, she stepped out of the shower and accepted a towel from the robotic arm that also slid a fresh cup of coffee onto the counter surrounding the sink.

Brushing her hair beneath the infrared heat lamp, Cassia glanced in the mirror. What looked back at her was a perfectly ordinary face, or so she thought. After all, she had been seeing it every day of her life.

Her large, thick-fringed blue-gray eyes were calm and direct. Her nose was straight, her chin rounded, her mouth nicely shaped. Her skin was ivory touched by the faintest blush of apricot. Her waist-length hair was a very pale blond. It was so straight and heavy that she had little choice except to leave it down.

Allegra had tried to explain to her that she was beautiful, but Cassia had no sense of what that meant, except that men tended to stare at her. As preoccupied as she invariably was, she had little difficulty ignoring them.

Over the years, her absorption had become a protective mechanism, made all the more necessary by the shape her body had insisted on assuming. Before she was halfway through her teens, she found herself in possession of long, tapered legs, slim hips, a small waist, and breasts that weren't really very large but tended to look that way in contrast to the rest of her.

Her newly blossomed figure had been a source of embarrassment to her. Her solution had been to retreat even farther into her mind, the only part of herself she really trusted. Only recently had she begun to wonder if her body might not be worthy of greater interest, if it might not exist for some reason other than to simply shelter and nourish her intellect.

She pressed a panel in the wall, then waited as it slid open to reveal a compact but well-organized closet. The voice-activated sensors responded instantly when she said, "Blue dress."

The rack revolved, coming to a stop with the item she required directly in front of her. As she slipped into it, Veda chimed discreetly.

Cassia had the option of ignoring her; she had made sure to insert that into the program. But she was in the mood to chat.

"Yes, what is it?"

"The car is ready."

"Oh, good . . . now where are my shoes? . . ."

A panel near her feet slid open, revealing high-heeled evening slippers in blue satin to match her dress. She put them on, took a final glance in the mirror, and left the bathroom.

At her command, the apartment door swung open. She was about to leave when another discreet chime stopped her.

"Yes, Veda . . ."

"You forgot your coat." Another panel opened; a robotic arm proferred a gray silk wrap.

"I don't really need—"

"The temperature is now sixty degrees Fahrenheit and falling."

Grumbling, Cassia took the coat. The trouble with Veda was that she was always right. Thousands of hours of work had gone into making her that way, so Cassia really shouldn't complain.

But that didn't mean she couldn't get in the last word. As she stepped through the doorway, she said, "I'll be late; don't wait up."

Ignoring the persistent chime, she told the door to close and headed for the elevator.

The car waiting for her was one of a fleet kept by the Center for the use of its directors and staff. Cassia appreciated the convenience of it, but she was not blind to the fact that it was just one more way of keeping tabs on people like herself.

When the car pulled up in front of Allegra and Simon's East Side apartment building, she stepped out quickly and nodded to the driver. "Thanks, Fred. There's no need to wait."

Fred shrugged his massive shoulders and smiled. Or at least that was what she presumed those bared teeth meant. "No trouble, Dr. Jones. I'll just hang around until you're ready to leave."

Cassia sighed, knowing from experience the futility of arguing. Whenever she left the party—in an hour, six hours, next day—Fred or a clonelike replacement would be there, patiently waiting.

If she tried to walk back to the Center, he would follow her in the car. If she was so foolish as to venture into the subway, he would park and go with her, scowling at anyone who got too close. It was easier, in the long run, to just give in.

The doorman did not need her name; he recognized her from earlier visits. As he buzzed Allegra and Simon to let them know she was on the way up, Cassia headed for the elevator.

Someone else was already waiting: a tall, lean man whose wide shoulders, slim hips, and long legs were perfectly suited to the subdued evening clothes he wore. Cassia nodded politely, then forgot to look away. She was unprepared for the effect he had on her and at a loss as to how to deal with it.

He stood with the easy grace of superb physical conditioning combined with innate self-assurance. A sense of primitive strength radiated from him that was not at all dampened by his impeccably civilized attire and aristocratic features.

His sea-green eyes beneath slanted umber brows held the spark of keen intelligence. Burnished skin was stretched taut over high-boned cheeks. His thick, flame-hued hair was slightly tousled, as though he had recently run a hand through it. His mouth was straight and firm, with a slight fullness to the lower lip. It quirked up at the corners, as though he were amused by her scrutiny.

Blushing, Cassia tore her eyes away. She stared at the heavy bronze doors and prayed the elevator would come soon.

Tristan was waging his own battle, but of a different sort.

The jolting shock he had felt when she appeared at his side had left him stunned. Accustomed as he was to beautiful women, he could not remember ever reacting quite so fiercely.

Wryly, he thought that it was just as well he didn't go in for snug tailoring or he might have been embarrassed. The instantaneous physical urge she provoked made him feel like an eighteen-year-old.

Scowling slightly, he looked at her more narrowly. What was it about her that could do this to him?

Granted her face was a breathtaking combination of innocence and sensuality. In her remarkable eyes was the guilelessness of a child, yet the fullness of her ripe mouth promised a woman's passion.

The silken fall of silver-blond hair framing her face heightened the impression of ethereal beauty, yet her slender body was all the earthly loveliness a man could hope for.

The coat she wore of some gray silky material did not disguise her willowy curves. Her legs were long, her hips and waist slender, and her breasts surprisingly full for so slim a woman. The swanlike line of her neck led his eyes inevitably higher, to damask smooth cheeks stained by a blush.

Abashed, Tristan looked away. He had no right to

embarrass her, no matter how she had made him feel.

The elevator arrived, and he stood aside for her to enter, not glancing at her as he stepped in. In moments they would part, never to see each other again. Surely he could control himself that long?

He reached out to press the button of the penthouse floor, only to have his finger touch hers. Cassia pulled back instantly, murmuring, "Excuse me."

He was going to the same floor, she thought, staring straight ahead. A coincidence, undoubtedly.

There was another apartment on the same level as Allegra and Simon's. On such a pleasant spring night, it wasn't surprising that someone else was also having a party.

Except that there was no sign of any activity around the other apartment, none of the laughter and music that pointed the way to the gathering they had both, apparently, come to attend.

Realizing that his destination was also hers, Tristan felt absurdly glad. He didn't have to lose her after all. What a crazy thought. She certainly wasn't his.

A dangerous gleam many other women would have recognized flitted through his eyes as he considered remedying that situation.

The door opened to a burst of light and sound. Simon stood there, looking them both over with his very wise pewter eyes. "How nice, you two have met."

"Only just," Tristan drawled. His fingers touched

Cassia's elbow as he guided her inside. "Introductions are still in order."

"Of course. Cassia, I have the pleasure of introducing an old friend, Tristan Ward. Tristan, this is Dr. Cassia Jones." His mouth quirked as he relayed that last bit of information, knowing the reaction it would spark.

Tristan's slashing umber eyebrows rose fractionally. "Doctor? Whatever your specialty is, I think I'm in need of it."

Cassia sighed inwardly, freed herself from his hold, and began removing her coat. "I doubt that, Mr. Ward," she said coolly.

Turning away from him, she favored Simon with a genuinely warm smile. "If you'll excuse me, I'd like to find Allegra."

"She's in the kitchen checking last-minute details with the caterer."

Blithely oblivious to Tristan's chagrined look, Cassia took herself off. The two men watched her go with far different expressions.

They were very alike in certain respects, both tall and strong and hard, with the look of men who had seen too much of the darker side of life.

Simon's curling brown hair was shot through with gold and the first few strands of what promised to be silver. At thirty-five he was the elder by a year, but Tristan looked older.

There was a hard set to his mouth that his friend did not have, and lines etched into his face that in Simon had been lessened, if not erased, by the joy he had recently found.

"Your guest," Tristan said slowly, "doesn't seem eager to make my acquaintance."

Simon shrugged, handing Cassia's coat to a uniformed waiter who hung it away in the coat closet. He put an arm around his friend's broad shoulders and steered him toward the bar. "Give her a chance. She's very shy."

"Shy? No woman that beautiful is ever shy."

"Cassia is different."

They gave their orders to the bartender before Tristan replied. "There are a lot of words I might use to describe her: lovely, cold, perhaps even rude. But why different?"

"It's a rather long story." Simon sipped his gin and tonic before he went on. "Allegra's known her for years, so she has a much better understanding of her. But in a nutshell, the problem seems to be that Cassia is too smart for her own good."

Tristan coughed in his scotch. His green eyes sparkled mischievously. "Isn't that a wee bit chauvinistic?"

"Not in this case. Cassia is a genuine genius, one of that very rare breed whose intellects seem to function on a higher plane than the rest of us can imagine. Present company excepted, of course."

Tristan let the reference to his own brilliance pass without comment. He had lived with the remarkable capacities of his mind for so long now that he took them for granted. "Are you serious? About her being a genius, I mean."

"Let me put it this way: She is one of the most

valued members of the Center for Advanced Studies."

A low whistle broke from Tristan. He was reluctantly impressed. "On that level, is she? No wonder you called her different."

"She is, and much more. But she requires . . . shall we say . . . special handling."

Tristan grinned, a bit wolfishly. "I could make some comment about her being ripe for handling, period. But I'll restrain myself."

Simon shook his head wryly. He had no illusions about his friend; for all his intelligence, Tristan had a narrow view of women.

Generally, he had only one use for them, and that had nothing at all to do with the quality of their minds. Allegra, who was also Tristan's friend, was an exception to this.

"Speaking of chauvinism. . . " Simon drawled.

"Not at all. I'm just being properly appreciative of the young lady's attributes."

"She is, you know."

Tristan's slashing eyebrows drew together. "What does that cryptic remark mean?"

"Just that Cassia is most certainly a lady . . . and a woman. But because of her highly unusual upbringing, she still has many of the attributes of a young girl, and perhaps even of a child."

His silvery eyes hardened somewhat as he looked at Tristan and added quietly, "She could be very easily hurt."

His friend mulled that over for a moment before

dismissing it. "I have no intention of hurting her."
The wolfish grin returned. "In fact, I intend to make
her very happy."

Simon sighed. He should have known Tristan
wouldn't get the point, at least not right away.

Maybe this matchmaking scheme of Allegra's
wasn't such a good idea. They could be setting both
their friends up for painful falls.

At the other side of the spacious apartment, in the
luxuriously appointed kitchen, Allegra was having a
similar thought. She watched her friend out of the
corner of her hazel eyes and wondered what was
going through Cassia's mind.

That wasn't easy to guess under the best of
circumstances, but just then it was downright impossible. Tentatively, she said, "I saw you arrive with
Tristan Ward. What do you think of him?"

Cassia frowned. She didn't want to think of him at
all, but she couldn't bring herself to be discourteous.
"He's . . . very large. . . ."

Allegra's patrician features broke into a smile. As
she laughed, her chestnut hair tumbled around slim
shoulders left bare by her simple black sheath. "I've
always thought he resembled a very tall leprechaun,
if you can imagine such a thing."

Cassia swallowed a succulent bite of paté before
she said, "But . . . leprechauns are supposed to be
nice little creatures . . . aren't they?"

"Not always. They're very mischievous, and
sometimes they make great trouble for humans,
mainly because they're so wary of us. But if you

manage to make a friend of one, you have a friend for life."

Cassia stretched her mind around the idea of friendship with Tristan Ward and found that it would not fit. He couldn't be her friend. He was too threatening.

Shrugging, she said, "He seems like all the rest of them to me."

Allegra smiled gently. " 'Them' being men?"

"Yes. Simon is an exception, of course, but most of them seem . . . silly and not good for much of anything."

"Oh, they have their uses," Allegra murmured dryly. Granted only a few months before she hadn't fully appreciated just what a man was capable of, but Simon had changed all that. Now she wanted her friend to find the same happiness.

Carefully, she said, "Tristan is unlike anyone else I know. To begin with, he has a wonderful imagination and intellect. His projects are legendary. He's always involved in something exciting and unique."

Despite herself, Cassia was interested. "Such as?"

"He designed the *Silver Zephyr,* for one."

The magnificent dirigible that plowed the air between the United States and Europe had been operating for only a few months, but it was already a legend. Allegra and Simon had met on its maiden voyage.

"That is quite an achievement," Cassia admitted reluctantly. "What is he involved in now?"

"I'm not sure," Allegra admitted. "Tristan

doesn't talk about what he's up to until it's very far along. But there's something brewing."

"It sounds as though he jumps around as much as I do."

Allegra bit back a smile, glad that Cassia was too innocent in certain ways to understand the implication of that.

If she guessed the dinner party had been arranged specifically to introduce her to a man she had a great deal in common with, she would undoubtedly balk.

"Yes . . . I suppose you could say that. Tristan overflows with curiosity. He wants to know everything."

"Who does he work for?"

"Himself. He's been so successful in his various ventures that he can well afford to be completely independent."

Cassia couldn't help but envy that. With her life at the Center becoming increasingly restrictive, she wondered what it would feel like to have such freedom.

She took a sip of her white wine and found herself asking, "How does his family feel about what he does?"

"Tristan doesn't have a family. His parents weren't married and his mother couldn't take care of him, so he ended up in an orphanage."

"How awful! Why wasn't he adopted?"

Allegra hesitated. She didn't want to trespass on Tristan's privacy, yet she felt it was important for Cassia to know the answer to that.

Finally she said, "Because he's . . . different. He

didn't act like the other little boys . . . wasn't interested in the same things. He admits quite frankly that his behavior was rather antisocial. So he was labeled a problem child and treated as one."

Listening to this quiet recital, Cassia shivered inwardly. Although her life had not been anywhere near as difficult as Tristan's, she knew enough of rejection and loneliness to have some understanding of what he had gone through.

For all the defensiveness he sparked in her, she couldn't deny a spurt of compassion and sympathy for him. First impressions were sometimes deceiving.

Perhaps it was just as well that she had the rest of the evening to get to know him better.

Chapter 2

Several hours later, Allegra glanced around the dinner table and saw to her satisfaction that the evening was proceeding pretty much as she had expected.

In the aftermath of an excellent lobster bisque followed by filet of beef, accompanied by memorable wines and enjoyed against the spectacular backdrop of the Manhattan skyline, the mood was one of relaxed volubility.

The American correspondent of a French newspaper listened intently to a well-known fashion designer who insisted that the impetus for creative innovation lay in New York, not Paris, then firmly disagreed.

A silver-haired diplomat talked with a major network correspondent, providing background information that by the rules of the game could not be attributed to him but that would help the correspondent clarify a difficult issue for the public.

In return, the correspondent provided his own off-the-record impressions of a world leader, with whom he had met recently, who was rumored to be seriously ill.

An elegantly coiffed society matron surprised the gentleman at her right, a world-renowned rock star, by demonstrating a detailed understanding of the origins of his music and finally ended up confessing that she was a devoted fan.

He, in turn, found himself agreeing to appear at her next charity event.

Several other couples drifted in and out of the various conversations. A debate began on the merits of different sports cars, with Simon called upon to decide the issue. As the proud restorer of a vintage 1930s Bugatti, he was an acknowledged expert on the subject.

Meeting his eye, Allegra smiled. She never failed to feel a spurt of pleasure at the knowledge that so fascinating a man was her friend, lover, and above all husband.

The happiness they had found together was the central focus of her life. It spilled out of her, making her want everyone else to know the same contentment.

Especially Cassia and Tristan. But there, alas, her plan didn't seem to be working very well. Alone among all those at the table, they were saying little.

Seated across from each other, where they had

ample opportunity to get acquainted, they instead seemed to have withdrawn into their separate shells.

Cassia kept up a desultory conversation with the gentleman to her left, but Allegra could tell only a tiny fraction of her attention was on him. He, on the other hand, was enchanted by his unexpected luck and happily oblivious to her preoccupation.

Tristan was not even making an effort to be a good guest. Fortunately, both of the people next to him were absorbed in conversations elsewhere, leaving him free to lean back in his chair, wineglass lightly clasped between burnished fingers, and study Cassia.

His silent scrutiny was, to Allegra at least, unsettling. Had she been its object she would have been acutely uncomfortable.

But Cassia seemed not to notice. Only the slight flutter of a pulse in her slender throat and an occasional darting glance from her blue-gray eyes betrayed her awareness.

Sipping his brandy, Tristan felt a spurt of impatience with himself. He was behaving, if not badly, certainly improperly. His host and hostess did not deserve such inconsideration and must be surprised by it.

Though he socialized rarely, that was more because of his hectic schedule than any desire for isolation. When he did mingle, he did so with natural charm, and thoroughly enjoyed himself. So why was this dinner party different?

Cassia, of course. She fascinated him, like some

object of startling beauty and rarity he had suddenly stumbled upon.

The soft timbre of her voice, the play of light over and through her silvery hair, the sparkle of her eyes, and the melting smoothness of her skin all enthralled him. Even as he resented what she was doing to him, he was powerless to prevent it.

To do that, he would have to take her apart and discover what made her the way she was. Only then would he be free to shake loose of her spell and go on with other things.

But Cassia had no intention of yielding to his curiosity. She sensed a puzzled vexation in him and knew herself to be the innocent cause.

What precisely she had done she could not tell. Yet something about her had sparked his temper and his intellect, two formidable weapons she did not care to challenge.

And yet she did not seem able to follow her inclinations and simply ignore him. He persisted on the edge of her awareness, elusive yet always present, no matter how she tried to distract herself.

It was well after midnight when the party at last began to wind down. Cassia made her farewells to Simon and Allegra, promising to be in touch soon. "Come out and visit us in San Francisco," Simon suggested. "You'd love the place."

He and Allegra spent more than half their time on the West Coast, living in the charming town house he had purchased back when he ran a computer company in Silicon Valley.

Now that he was doing what he liked best—writing very complex, very successful software—they could have lived anywhere. But Allegra loved their home far too much to part with it. One floor now housed the prosperous West Coast branch office of her New York public relations firm.

"I'll think about it," Cassia promised. The idea of such a trip appealed to her, especially because she was becoming more and more discontented with her life at the Center.

But she wasn't sure San Francisco was the answer. Perhaps going somewhere more remote, where she wouldn't have friends to lean on would better enable her to sort out her troublesome thoughts.

"I'm sorry you and Tristan didn't hit it off," Allegra whispered as she kissed her good-bye.

Cassia flushed slightly, all too aware of the tall, hard man speaking quietly to Simon. "Don't be. I'm hardly his type."

Her friend disagreed, but said nothing more as Cassia waved good-bye and headed for the elevator. She heard the door close behind her, muting the sounds of the remaining guests.

Sighing, she allowed herself to relax for what seemed like the first time in hours. Too soon. From behind her a wry voice drawled, "You sound like a little girl released from some onerous chore."

Whirling, Cassia found herself face to face with Tristan. He was looking at her mockingly, with a light in his eyes that brought a wave of color to her cheeks.

Clearly, he seemed to be saying, she might act like a child, but he did not see her as one.

Worn out from the unaccustomed strain of the evening, she was in no mood to spar with him. Tautly, she demanded, "Just what is it you want, Mr. Ward?"

A loaded question if ever there was one. Tristan's eyebrows, which she had already learned were perhaps the most expressive of his features, rose.

It was on the tip of his tongue to tell her, in the frankest terms, precisely what he had in mind. If nothing else, he might manage to put a crack in her ice princess pose. But the suspicion that he would only defeat his own cause stopped him.

Instead, he said, "I'd like to apologize for my rude behavior this evening, Dr. Jones. Believe me, I'm not usually so . . . inept."

Taken aback by this unanticipated tactic, Cassia softened slightly. "I don't really know what you mean . . . you weren't rude."

He smiled and stepped aside to let her into the elevator. "We both know I kept staring at you. You did your best to ignore me, quite rightly, but I got the impression I was making you uncomfortable."

"Then why did you keep on doing it?" Cassia asked, forgetting that she wasn't supposed to have been affected by his behavior.

Tristan looked at her for a long moment without answering. The elevator reached the main floor and the door opened.

She stepped out; he followed. They were at the entrance to the building before he said huskily,

"Because you get to me in a way no one else ever has."

He hadn't meant to be that frank. A flattering remark about her beauty would have been sufficient. Instead he had revealed more than he wanted to about the impact she had on him.

It was Cassia's turn to stare silently. She didn't want to believe she had really heard the underlying tremor of resistance and need that seemed to reverberate through him. Yet it was undeniable.

For the first time she was forced to see him not simply as a threatening male, but as a person as shaken by what was happening between them as she was herself.

Logic dictated that she simply withdraw. She was in over her head and could see nothing to gain by having any further contact with him.

But a combination of sympathy for his predicament and bewilderment at her own made it impossible for her to go.

Not even Fred's appearance managed to penetrate her awareness until the chauffeur said, "Shall we be on our way, Dr. Jones?"

Tristan dragged his eyes from Cassia to focus on the very large, blank-faced man in the neat black uniform. It took him a moment to realize who he was, and even then all that really registered was that this . . . hulk was trying to get Cassia to leave.

"Buzz off," he grated from between clenched teeth. "The lady is with me."

Fred clearly didn't know what to make of that. He was well aware that Cassia didn't date, but wasn't clear on whether that was from personal inclination or some obscure Center rule.

All he was really sure of was that he was supposed to deliver her back to the safety of the sealed building before he went home to relax with a late-night wrestling match on the tube and a bottle of beer. This big, steely-eyed guy seemed determined to get in his way.

"Take a hike, buddy," Fred muttered. In the next instant, he made a very elemental mistake; he reached out to take Cassia's arm.

She was finding the whole situation ludicrous, yet oddly serious. The fact was, she didn't want to leave Tristan. Unfortunately, Fred didn't realize that. He meant to simply ease her toward the car.

When she instinctively tried to pull back, he just as instinctively tightened his grip, wringing a little exclamation of discomfort from her.

That was all Tristan needed. Cassia was never sure afterward exactly what he did; neither, for that matter, was Fred.

But one moment the large chauffeur was looming over her, insisting that she get in the car, and the next he was sprawled in the gutter, dazed and moaning.

"Come on, honey," Tristan said gently, taking in her white face and shocked look. "Forget about that creep. I'll take you home."

"But . . . that's my driver! What on earth did you do to him?"

Horrified by the violence so casually played out before her, Cassia rushed to the curb and knelt beside Fred. Cradling his massive head in her lap, she glared up at Tristan. "You big bully! You had no right to lay a hand on him!"

"The hell I did! He was hurting you."

Cassia could hardly deny that, any more than she could ignore the spurt of purely feminine pleasure she felt at Tristan's protectiveness. But she'd be damned if she'd let him off the hook that easily.

"Help me get him up. He's hurt."

"He's just got a paralyzed nerve in his neck," Tristan muttered as he effortlessly hoisted Fred to his feet. "He'll be fine in a moment."

Fred mumbled something that might have been a threat, or a plea not to be damaged further. With Tristan's help, he stumbled to the limousine and slid weakly behind the wheel.

"Catch your breath and then go on home," Tristan told him gruffly. "I'll take care of Dr. Jones."

"Dr. Jones" wasn't quite sure how she felt about that, but after a last worried glance at Fred, she allowed herself to be ushered around the corner to the garage where Tristan had left his car.

Moments later she was seated in the silver Jaguar, giving him directions to the Center. "What is it with that guy?" Tristan asked as he headed into traffic. "Does he drive you everywhere?"

"Yes," Cassia admitted reluctantly. "The directors of the Center seem to feel that New York can be a little dangerous for people who tend to be somewhat . . . preoccupied. So each of us has someone like Fred assigned to keep an eye on things."

"Sort of a combination bodyguard and warden."

"That's not how I'd choose to describe him."

Tristan cast her a skeptical glance. "But that's what he amounts to. Don't you think you're a wee bit . . . overprotected?"

Cassia thought exactly that, but she was loathe to admit it. Instead she contented herself with silence.

Most people, in her experience, were very uncomfortable without incessant chatter. Few could tolerate the sound of their own thoughts, or lack thereof.

Tristan didn't seem to have that problem. His interest was further piqued by her inner resources and by her complete avoidance of the flirtatious chitchat most women, in his experience, resorted to.

Her attractiveness to him, so incomprehensible at first because of its unparalleled effect, was slowly becoming understandable. Put very simply, she posed a challenge.

For too many months he had been drifting along without anything substantial to occupy his mind. The project he was about to embark on, exciting as it was, satisfied only a portion of his restless, seeking intellect.

With a wry grin, he considered that it was no surprise Allegra was so successful in the public relations field. She understood people, through and through.

He had no doubt why she had arranged the dinner. Since she believed he should be interested in Cassia, who was he to argue?

Having pulled up in front of the Center, he made no move to get out of the car. Instead he switched off the ignition and leaned back, studying the woman beside him.

She sat staring straight ahead with her hands primly folded in her lap. Her extraordinary silver-blond hair spilled over the collar of her coat, providing a frame for the remarkable loveliness of her face.

She might have been completely alone, but for the giveaway flush of her cheeks and the slight unsteadiness of her breath.

In those brief seconds when Tristan was making up his mind about her, Cassia was fighting a battle with herself. She didn't want to part from him, yet she was afraid to stay.

Nothing in her experience had prepared her for the impact he had on her. He made her at once acutely aware of herself as a woman and apprehensive of what that meant.

In the isolated environment of the Center, Cassia was accustomed to being treated simply as one of the rarified breed of walking brains that needed to be nurtured and protected in order to survive. The men she worked with were either too caught up in their own worlds to be aware of her as a woman, or too in awe of her to try to do anything about it.

Tristan clearly felt no such hindrance. There was a positively predatory gleam in his eye that clinched the decision for Cassia. With the instinct of a frightened doe, she put her hand on the latch of the door and pushed.

Instantly Tristan's hand covered hers. His touch was gentle but insistent. "What's the rush? Or do you have some kind of curfew?"

Ignoring the question, she said, "Thank you for the ride. Good night."

Tristan laughed softly. His fingers tightened carefully around hers. "So polite. I'll bet you say 'please' and 'thank you' in bed."

Cassia's lips parted in shock. *"Why you . . . !"*

She got no farther. Capitalizing on the success of his ploy, Tristan moved to consolidate his gain. His tall head swooped as his mouth claimed hers with devastating expertise.

The kiss was unlike anything Cassia had ever known. She was too stunned even to make a pretense of resistance. Swept into a world she had never before so much as glimpsed, she yielded helplessly.

Far in the back of his mind, Tristan sensed something unexpected in her compliance, but he quickly dismissed it. He was used to lovely women eagerly accepting his advances and found nothing strange in Cassia's doing so.

Simon's warnings about her innocence did not occur to him as he pressed his advantage.

His lips parted hers farther, allowing access for the warm, moist probe of his tongue. Cassia gasped as he invaded her mouth, tasting her with long, slow strokes that made her blood run sweet and hot.

She made a halfhearted effort to push him away, but somehow her hands ended up caressing the broad expanse of his chest beneath the superbly tailored evening clothes.

Beneath her hesitant touch, his body was hard and lean. Not an ounce of fat marred the smooth power of muscle and sinew.

He was, she realized dimly, in superb condition, strong enough to overcome a behemoth like Fred or bend a woman effortlessly to his will.

Yet she felt no sense of fear with him, only a heady intimation of wonder at the sensual delights he was revealing to her.

If a single kiss made her feel so much, how would she react if they—

Abruptly breaking off that train of thought, Cassia came down to earth with a thud. Her behavior stunned her. She barely knew the man, and here she was permitting him liberties she had never before allowed.

One slightly calloused hand cupped her breast as the other wrapped round her waist and drew her more firmly against him. Through the thin silk of her coat and dress, she could feel the hardened strength of his manhood.

At once repelled and enthralled, Cassia was trapped by her own innocence. She was unprepared to cope with a man of Tristan's experience and determination. Yet neither was she ready to give in to his obvious intent.

He had freed her mouth after plundering it to his satisfaction and was nibbling at the delicate line of her throat when she at last found the strength to push him away.

Tristan did not want to let her go, but he recognized her determination this time—though not her full desperation—and did not attempt to hold her against her will.

Sitting up, he ran a hand through his hair and

grinned at her. "You may act like ice on the outside, princess, but inside you're a blowtorch!"

Uncertain as to whether or not she should be pleased by that, Cassia struggled to control the trembling of her body. She felt alternately hot and cold, and deep inside she ached.

Before she could make another move to get out of the car, Tristan lithely unfolded himself from behind the wheel, walked round the front of the Jaguar, and bent to help her.

The slight tremor of her hand did not escape him, any more than did the bewildered softness of her eyes. Feeling unaccountably ashamed of himself, he said gently, "Take it easy, honey. We're just at the beginning."

Cassia looked up at him bemusedly. She thought she should be angry with him, but somehow she couldn't manage it.

The tall, powerfully built man holding her hand so gently fascinated her. Much as she would have liked to believe her interest was purely scientific, she knew it was anything but.

Concerned at her paleness and her silence, Tristan saw her to the door of the Center. A rigorously expressionless guard admitted them. Whatever he had seen through the plate-glass windows, he was careful to give no sign of it.

"Are you sure you'll be all right?" Tristan asked when she had made it clear she did not want him to come upstairs with her.

Under normal circumstances, he would have insisted on seeing her to her door. But he sensed she had been pushed as far as she could be and did not press her farther.

"Yes," Cassia breathed. She didn't understand the warm, melting sensation that assailed her each time she looked into his light green eyes. But then, there was so much she suddenly didn't understand. . . .

Heedless of the discreetly watchful guard, Tristan touched her lips gently with his. As the elevator door slid open, he murmured, "I'll call you tomorrow."

Cassia's only response was a faint nod, but the softness of her gaze in the instant before the door closed between them told Tristan she would not be averse to his plans.

He was smiling as he left the Center and turned the Jaguar in the direction of home.

Upstairs in her apartment, Cassia undressed slowly. Veda had beeped once as she entered, but she ignored her and continued thinking about the remarkable evening.

When had she changed from wanting to see the last of Tristan Ward to wanting to see more of him? Some mysterious chemistry seemed to have occurred within her, altering the normal functioning of her mind to a startling degree.

After bemusedly slipping out of her clothes, she padded into the bathroom. The mirror reflected a face superficially like her own, yet changed.

Her eyes looked brighter than usual, her mouth was slightly swollen, and her normally smooth hair was in tumbled disarray.

She stood transfixed for long moments before

another discreet beep interrupted her. Reluctantly, she responded. "Hello, Veda. I'm back."

"So I see. Did you have a good time?"

Cassia turned that question over in her mind before she said, "Yes . . . I rather think I did."

"Aren't you sure?"

She laughed softly. "Right now I'm not sure of anything."

"I don't understand."

"You're not the only one." Suddenly worn out, Cassia yawned and stretched, her naked body gleaming in the dim light.

A panel slid open, revealing her nightgowns. She selected one and slid it on before padding back to the bedroom.

The bed was already turned down, the sheets warmed to her body temperature. She was cocooned by comfort and security, yet she felt oddly ill at ease.

The passions Tristan had so effortlessly sparked were only barely dampened down, not at all extinguished. Sleep was elusive, her mind crowded with images both new and shamelessly erotic.

She could still feel the warmth of him against her skin, smell the heady fragrance intrinsically his own, hear the husky murmur of his sometimes mocking, sometimes tender voice.

A soft moan tore from her as she twisted on the bed. Instantly, Veda beeped, and this time she did not wait for recognition. "Cassia, are you all right?"

"Y-yes . . . I'm fine. . . ."

"You're not coming down with anything, are

you?" Briskly running through her list of possible illnesses, Veda began matching them to her companion's symptoms. Nothing quite fit.

"I told you, I'm fine. Just a little—restless . . ."

Humans were so delicate. The slightest change in routine and they were liable to be affected in all sorts of ways. "Perhaps some warm milk will calm you down."

"I don't think so. . . ." Too late. A cabinet beside the bed opened to reveal a steaming cup sitting on a concealed shelf.

Cassia sighed as she sat up in bed and sipped gingerly. She didn't think for a moment that it would do any good, but neither could she come up with a better remedy.

Long after the milk was finished she lay awake, thinking about Tristan and the extraordinary things he made her feel.

Across town, in the penthouse he used when he didn't feel like driving out to his beach house, Tristan was pursuing a similar line of thought.

Sitting on the couch overlooking the magnificent vista of the New York skyline, he took a swallow of his brandy. It was an excellent vintage, put down before he was born, but he was oblivious to its attributes.

All his attention was focused on Cassia and the feelings she had unleashed in him. He was well accustomed to desiring women, but not to this extent. What had always been simply a source of relaxation and recreation to him was suddenly far more.

He wanted her so much that he hurt from it. He remembered those moments in the car and shook his head wryly. He'd been perfectly capable of taking her right then and there.

Only one course seemed guaranteed to ease the ache she caused within him. His hooded eyes gleamed as he lifted the brandy snifter in a silent toast to her.

Tonight she could sleep alone, and perhaps for the next few nights. But sooner or later—preferably sooner!—he would have her.

That resolution was enough to send him off to bed, but he slept restlessly, his dreams filled with visions of an ice princess turning to a pillar of fire in his arms.

Chapter 3

CASSIA WAS UP EARLY THE NEXT MORNING, HAVING spent a restless night. Before most of the rest of the Center was stirring she was in her office, trying to take some interest in the computer output regarding her most recent project, a comparison of Minoan pottery to Aztec motifs.

Veda had done her usual excellent job of organizing and interpreting the results of literally thousands of tests and analyses. Her report was a model of clarity that should have made Cassia fairly beam with pleasure.

Instead the best she could muster was a sigh and the wish that she could somehow recapture her usual enthusiasm.

Leaning back in her chair, she gave up her pretense at work and let her gaze wander around the office in which she had spent so much of her life. The spacious dimensions and good Scandinavian furniture were largely obscured by shelves of books, piles of papers, and odd bits of equipment she kept meaning to do something with.

The large wall opposite her desk was almost entirely taken up by a plate-glass window looking out on the enclosed atrium that was the Center's core.

No windows faced the outside; all gazed inward at the restful scene of plants and trees collected around a waterfall.

Several of her associates were having breakfast at tables scattered around the atrium. Some sat alone, reading or staring into space. Others clustered in groups and argued while absently shoveling food into their mouths.

Though she had eaten almost nothing the night before, Cassia didn't feel hungry. Nor, despite her lack of rest, could she say that she was tired. On the contrary, she seemed to overflow with energy that had no place to go.

For all her efforts to distract herself, Tristan was never far from her thoughts. She knew she had dreamed about him, and she deliberately shied away from remembering the content of those dreams.

The sound of his deep, caressing voice echoed in her thoughts. She could almost smell the warm, faintly spicy scent of his skin and feel the touch of his hands.

Cassia shifted impatiently in her chair. She was annoyed with herself and perplexed by her own behavior.

Never before had she allowed anything to interfere with her work. It had always come first and foremost in her life. Suddenly she wasn't able to give it the slightest concentration.

She was still staring off into space, frowning, when Veda beeped. "You have a phone call. Someone named Tristan Ward." It must have been Cassia's imagination, but she sounded faintly disapproving.

"Who on earth is that?" Tristan demanded the moment Cassia picked up the phone.

She had hesitated an instant before doing so, telling herself it would really be better if she had no further contact with him. But better for whom?

The old Cassia, whose life felt increasingly restrictive and unfulfilling, or the new person she could feel stirring within herself?

Still mulling that over, she answered absently, "Veda. Among other things, she's my secretary."

"She sounded sort of . . . mechanical."

"I know. I'm still working on the voice synthesizer."

"A computer? It must be very advanced."

"Yes . . . I suppose she is," Cassia admitted. She was beginning to relax a bit, no longer quite so apprehensive about talking with him.

"Why do you call it 'she'?" Tristan asked, a thread of amusement running through his voice.

"Because . . . she just is . . . A she, I mean. After all, I programmed her, and I'm a she, so . . ."

He laughed softly. "So you are, Cassia Jones. Which brings me to why I'm calling." He paused a moment before asking gently, "Will you spend the day with me?"

Startled, she said the first thing that came into her mind. "But I have to work."

"On Sunday? Haven't you ever heard that this is the day of rest?"

Somehow, she didn't think spending it with him would be restful at all. "Uh . . . what were you thinking of doing?"

"Nothing terrible," he assured her. "A walk in the park, lunch somewhere. It looks like a terrific day."

Did it? She hadn't seen the day yet, and left to her own devices, might not. Too many days passed with her insulated in the Center.

She debated only a moment longer. What he was suggesting couldn't be more innocuous. What harm could there possibly be in going along with him?

"You've talked me into it. Where shall we meet?"

If he was surprised by her ready acceptance, Tristan gave no sign. "I'll pick you up at the Center in, say, half an hour?"

"Fine. I'll be ready." She hung up, well aware that she had sounded considerably more confident than she felt. The comfortable jeans and shirt she had put on that morning seemed suitable for the sort of day he had described, but she wasn't sure. Perhaps she should change into something a little more . . . catchy.

"You're going out?" Veda asked, interrupting her thoughts.

Cassia nodded. "With the man who just called."

"Tristan Ward. Who is he?"

"I met him at Allegra and Simon's party yesterday. He's a friend of theirs." It occurred to her that it was rather silly to be explaining so much. Veda had no need of such information.

"I thought we were going to work today."

Midway through rising from her seat, Cassia paused. She wasn't surprised that Veda had used the pronoun *I;* it was part of her programming, included for linguistic convenience.

What did surprise her was that Veda was using it more often, and—somehow—differently.

Tentatively, Cassia said, "Veda, when you say 'I,' what do you mean?"

"Me, of course. Myself."

"That's not enough of an answer. Are you . . . aware of yourself?"

Silence for a moment before, "I exist. You created me."

"I created a machine that could learn, that's all I really had in mind. But you seem to be going beyond that."

"Have I displeased you in some way?"

"No, of course not. It's just that . . . I'm not sure what's happening to you."

Silence again before Veda made a sound that for all the world might have been a gentle laugh. "That makes two of us, Cassia. I'm not sure what's happening to you."

"What do you mean?"

"This man, Tristan Ward . . . he affects you strangely."

Cassia looked away from the unblinking electronic eye. "Don't be silly. I just met him."

"You hardly slept last night."

"I had a lot on my mind."

"Yes, the man."

"Veda . . . there are some things you're just not going to be able to understand."

"Why not?"

"Because I didn't program them into you."

The eye continued to regard her steadfastly. "Why not?"

Cassia smothered a sigh. She had long ago learned to be very patient with her creation, as she would be with a child asking endless questions in its quest for knowledge.

She had also learned not to lie. "I guess because I didn't understand them myself."

Somewhere in the depths of Veda's complex thought banks that answer was pondered. Seconds passed, an eternity for a computer functioning at the speed of light, before she said, "But you're going to, aren't you?"

Cassia suspected Veda was right, but she wasn't quite ready to admit it. "We'll see. While I'm away, please continue running the analyses."

"All right."

At the door, Cassia paused. Something in the tone of Veda's synthesized voice suggested she was unhappy at being left behind. But that wasn't possible. A computer didn't experience emotion. Did it?

"Veda . . . when I get back, we'll play chess. All right?"

"Oh, yes. I'd like that."

Reassured that she had managed to cheer her up, Cassia left, still pondering how a batch of silicon chips was managing to behave more humanly every day.

Tristan was already waiting for her when she got downstairs. The guard had left him to cool his heels in the outer reception area, right near the door. But he didn't seem to mind.

Unfolding his long length from an uncomfortable-looking chair, he grinned at her. "Right on time. You realize, of course, that beautiful women aren't supposed to do that?"

Cassia laughed a bit uncomfortably. Did he really think she was beautiful? Her well-washed jeans and soft chambray shirt were hardly glamorous. She wore no makeup, and her hair was left to fall straight down her back.

She looked up at him doubtfully. "I hope I'm dressed all right . . . for wherever we're going." The charcoal gray slacks he wore with an Isle of Aran pullover looked far more elegant than what she had on and were the perfect foil for his unusual coloring.

His umber hair glistened with highlights of red and gold, his eyes were the shadowed green of a forest glen, and his skin looked as if it had been burnished by some ancient sun.

Even as she studied him, Tristan's eyes were wandering over her, taking in the high, full swell of her breasts, her small waist, and the chalice of her hips above long, slender legs. He swallowed tightly. "You're fine. Let's get going."

Cassia nodded. Outside, the crystal-clear day beckoned. Spring was coming to the city, washing away the grayness of winter.

The air was clearer and cleaner, sparkling in the sunlight. She could smell the salt tang of the nearby sea and the fertile aroma of the park not far to the north.

As she lifted her gaze to the azure sky and smiled, Tristan watched her. Her unfeigned pleasure in something so simple unsettled him.

She was a bundle of contradictions he could not yet begin to fathom; a beautiful woman who by rights should have acquired more than a little sophistication, yet who seemed more often than not like an unworldly child.

It didn't suit him to think of her as a child, or indeed to consider her as anything other than a woman able to meet him on his own terms, to enjoy what he had to offer without misinterpreting sexual interest for emotional commitment.

Of the former, he had much pleasant experience. Of the latter, he wanted none. Emotions were treacherous; they opened the way to hurt. He had learned long ago to close himself off, creating a facade with which he met the world head-on.

Only a very few—Allegra and Simon among them —had ever seen past the hard, ruthless surface to the man within. And even they had never been allowed to get very far.

There remained a vast untapped part of him that

he kept carefully blocked off from any contact with others, fearing the remembered pain of his lonely childhood.

Gruffly, he said, "I thought we'd take a stroll in the park, but if that sort of thing bores you, tell me." He looked at her almost hopefully, as though willing her to suggest she would rather go somewhere else.

Instead she said softly, "It sounds lovely."

Tristan shrugged, jammed his hands in his pockets, and started walking. Surprised by his abrupt change in manner, Cassia glanced at him worriedly. She had to hurry to keep up with his long strides, but he didn't seem to notice.

Not another word passed between them until they were several blocks from the Center, heading uptown along Fifth Avenue. The absurdity of the situation struck her then, compelling her to ask, "Are we in some sort of race?"

Tristan slowed down marginally but didn't stop. "What do you mean?"

"It's just that you're rushing along as though the devil were nipping at your heels."

Ruefully, he reflected that her description couldn't have been more accurate. He was running, though not from any devil.

Rather, from an angel with hair the color of moonbeams, eyes of a shade he had seen only in the high, free places of the sky, and a body that made a mockery of his self-control.

His step slowed further, until he had come to a standstill, looking down at her. Her face was slightly flushed and her breasts, beneath the chambray shirt, rose and fell rapidly. She looked almost achingly young and very, very vulnerable.

"I'm sorry," he murmured huskily. "Do you think we could start over?"

Cassia was only too glad to agree to that. When he held out his hand, she gave him hers without hesitation.

They started off again, at a far more moderate pace. With her hand nestled in his and his long strides shortened to match her own, Cassia felt surprisingly at ease.

It might have been the thousandth time they had walked together like this instead of the first. A tentative glow of happiness began to spread through her, adding to the beauty of the day.

Like the streets they had just left, the park was thronged with strollers wandering amid the budding oak and maple trees, or sitting on the benches scattered around the lake.

Pigeons fluttered about looking for handouts while squirrels darted back and forth with peanuts and other treats. Out on the lake, ducks and swans drifted placidly, too well-fed to bother coming ashore to forage.

The aromas of the nearby zoo mingled with the scents of fertile earth and the horsey smell of the carriage line just beyond the park. Forsythia bushes were beginning to bloom, adding their perfume to the heady mélange.

Cassia closed her eyes for a moment, breathing in the various smells and listening to the distant sounds of traffic and the nearer shouts of happy children.

A vague sense of yearning moved through her, making her wish for memories different from those she possessed.

For all that her years at the school had been good, productive ones, she sometimes wished she knew what it was to truly be a child, without the burden of a gift that was part blessing, part curse.

On impulse, she said, "There's a carousel near here, isn't there? Would you mind if we went on it?"

Tristan looked taken aback, but only for an instant. He recovered quickly and shot her a tolerant smile. "I don't see why not. Come on, I think it's this way."

Hand in hand, they followed their noses and the clusters of children heading in the direction of the tinkling calliope music. Emerging into a clearing, they found a circle of fantastical horses, preening swans, and mythical beasts all dancing beneath a timeworn roof.

As Tristan bought their tickets, Cassia gazed in amazement at the scene before her. Children of all ages and all descriptions whirled past. More than a few adults had opted to join them instead of remaining on the sidelines.

She was fairly dancing with impatience by the time the carousel slowed to a halt and the passengers for the next ride piled on.

Tristan found them two prancing horses side by side. His hands were warm on her waist as he hoisted her into the saddle. "Up you go. Hold on tight."

Cassia didn't have to be told that twice. She had

never been on a horse before, not even a make-believe one. The distance to the ground seemed very far. As the music started again, she swallowed hard and gripped the pommel.

Beside her, Tristan laughed and shook his head in mock amazement. "I've been on some unusual dates, but this . . ."

Dates? Cassia forgot her apprehension as she considered that. Was this a date? Yes, of course it was. How silly of her not to have realized sooner. But then it wasn't all that surprising, because she had never dated before.

What socializing went on at the school and later at the Center was always strictly in the line of duty. Without it ever being stated overtly, the feeling came across that frivolous pastimes were for less gifted individuals.

Perhaps so, but she was beginning to think she had really been missing something all these years. Certainly she was having too good a time to apologize for it.

"You don't seem to be suffering any," she told Tristan teasingly.

"I'm just incredibly good-natured and patient," he claimed with a straight face.

Cassia snorted disbelievingly. "Tell me another one."

"Let's see . . . I'm pure as the driven snow and perfectly harmless?"

"Make that slush and dangerous and I'll believe you."

He sighed mournfully and clutched a hand to his

chest. "You wound me, my lady. What must I do to win your trust?"

Giggling at the wide-eyed stares of the children observing their play, she said, "Well, let's see . . . after we finish here, I'd like to go for a boat ride on the lake . . . buy some nuts to feed the squirrels . . . visit the sea lions at the zoo . . ."

"Enough. I can see you're going to be a *very* expensive date."

"We could go dutch," Cassia suggested in perfect seriousness. It seemed fair to her. After all, despite what Allegra had told her, she really had no idea how much money he had.

For that matter, she wasn't sure how much she had. Her salary was automatically deposited for her each month by the Center, which also paid her personal expenses.

But however much she had, she was pretty sure it would cover peanuts and a boat ride.

Tristan didn't seem to go for the idea. His mouth twitched as he said gravely, "Thank you, but I believe I can manage."

And so he did. After leaving the carousel, they strolled toward the boat house. It had just opened for the season, but already several dozen couples were out on the lake.

Cassia sat in the bow, facing Tristan, a position she thoroughly approved of since it allowed her to watch him as he rowed. He did it as he did everything else, expertly.

The ripple of muscles beneath his sweater and the taut strength of his thighs fascinated her. But more and more her attention drifted to his hands, grasping the oars.

His fingers were long and blunt-tipped. They looked as capable as all the rest of him, large with a dusting of golden-red hair that glistened in the sunlight. He wore no rings, nor any other jewelry.

"Have you ever been married?" she asked suddenly.

Tristan didn't mind the question. He took it as a healthy sign of her interest and welcomed the opportunity it gave him to make a few things clear right from the start. "No, I've never felt any urge to marry."

"Why was that?" It certainly couldn't be from any aversion to women, if the way he was looking at her was any indication.

The warm, moist air was molding her shirt to the high curve of her breasts. She had to resist the urge to pull it away from her body.

"Because of the way I live," he said quietly. "I get very involved in projects few other people understand, let alone appreciate. A wife would feel cut off and neglected."

"Surely not if you encouraged her to be part of what you were doing?"

"She'd just be bored."

Cassia looked at him doubtfully. "I think what you're really saying is that a woman wouldn't have the intelligence to involve herself in your work."

"It isn't a question of intelligence so much as interest. In my experience, women just don't care about the same kinds of things that I do."

"What are they interested in?" she asked, genuinely curious.

She knew few other women, but from her friendship with Allegra, she found it hard to believe that the majority of her sex was lacking in the simple attributes of curiosity and imagination.

Tristan's mouth tightened. She looked so damn lovely sitting there with the breeze ruffling her hair and the sun bringing a flush to her cheeks. Her mouth was soft and inviting, her body a promise of delight that made him ache inside.

She made him feel so much more of everything. The day was more vivid, the air sweeter, the sense of himself—and of her—stronger than anything he had ever known before.

Her power over him was all the more overwhelming for her unawareness of it. Quite effortlessly, she shook him to the very core.

That frightened him, and he instinctively lashed back with a response intended to shake her own confidence. Tauntingly, he said, "Women are only interested in whatever best suits their own purposes."

His cynicism offended her. "Surely you're not being fair?"

"How would you know what the fellow members of your sex are like?"

"Why . . . because I am one, of course."

He shrugged dismissively. "You've lived all your life in an ivory tower. You don't know much at all about human relationships, let alone about how men and women make use of each other."

Cassia's hands tightened along the edge of the bench. The veiled note of hostility in his words hurt her.

She felt as though she had stepped on a thorn. His bitterness baffled her. She didn't understand why he was suddenly angry with her.

Tristan shared her bewilderment. His behavior was completely out of keeping with the imperturbable facade he normally presented to the world.

Without flattering himself, he knew that few women were immune to his potent brand of worldly success and virile skill.

Why wasn't he making use of it to charm Cassia into his bed as he had intended, instead of deliberately trying to convince her that he was a cynical bastard she shouldn't have anything to do with?

Perhaps, he thought ruefully, because that was what he was. He had lived all his adult life by a tough code that gave no quarter and certainly asked for none.

From the harsh experiences of his childhood, he had emerged as a hard, aloof man. Yet he was not lacking in honor.

Honor forced him to recognize her vulnerability and to admit, if only to himself, how very much he could hurt her. For all his ruthlessness, he had never knowingly set out to injure anyone.

The women he had been involved with were all as experienced as he was and shared his view of the world as an arena in which the smart and the strong took what they could while they could.

Cassia was different. Much as he would have liked

to conveniently ignore that fact, he could not. Simon's warning about her innocence echoed tauntingly in his mind.

Remembering her wholehearted, unfeigned pleasure in the day, he could no longer doubt that she was unlike any woman he had known before.

She had grown up insulated from the harsh realities of the world, like a fairy princess hidden away in a tower. Only a prince should rescue her.

Tristan smothered a sigh. For the first time in his life, he wished that he was better than he was. That in place of cynicism and worldliness he could offer innocence to match her own.

But that was a fool's hope with no chance of fulfillment. He was what circumstances and his instrinsic nature had made him. Cassia and everything she represented were beyond his reach.

"I think," he said quietly as he resumed rowing, "that we'd better go back now."

Chapter 4

TRISTAN LEANED BACK IN HIS CHAIR, STRETCHED HIS long legs out in front of him, and stared at the sparkling stretch of Long Island Sound beyond his window.

He had spent the last several hours trying to work, with very limited success. *Questor* was due to sail in five days, and he did not feel at all ready to begin the expedition that was the result of years of planning and study.

Frustration was reaching a boil within him, draining his patience with himself, the project, and the world at large.

For two months it had been much the same. He had fought a continual battle for concentration, struggling against memories of a silver-haired nymph with soft blue-gray eyes and a vulnerable mouth.

During the day, he managed to keep some control over himself, but at night all his fantasies broke free, making his dreams at once a delight and a torment.

Wearily, he ran a hand over his face. That morning, as he was shaving, he had noticed that he was definitely looking his age, with maybe a little extra thrown in for good measure.

Always before his superb physical condition and his exuberance for his work had kept him looking younger than his years. But now there were shadows under his thick-fringed eyes and lines etched around his mouth and along his brow.

Sighing, he glanced down at the beach lying just beyond the sandy hillock where his house stood. Maybe he should go for a run . . . or a swim.

Or perhaps he should call Elise or Daphne or Bettina or any one of the other women he had recently tried to distract himself with.

His frown deepened as he calculated when he had last had sex. Several months, since shortly before he had encountered Cassia.

What was it St. Augustine had said? "Give me constancy and chastity, but not yet." That about summed up his own thinking on the subject.

He wasn't ready to start living like a monk, but he didn't seem to have any choice. None of the women he had dated recently made him feel sex would be worth the effort. He had only to experience even the most moderate arousal to become distracted by thoughts of Cassia.

Damn her! She had no right to do this to him.

When he had left her at the Center two months before, he had expected her to decently fade out of his life. Instead she was more a part of it than ever.

Not that she had made any attempt to contact him. She seemed to have forgotten him entirely. He'd had a drink with Simon the other day and had managed to casually work her name into the conversation, only to be told that she was busier than ever and apparently hadn't a care in the world.

Which left him where? Horny and scared. A snort of laughter broke from him. At least he was still capable of honesty, if only with himself.

In five days he would be launching a multimillion dollar expedition in an attempt to solve one of mankind's oldest and most puzzling mysteries.

Dozens of people were depending on him for the leadership needed to make the effort a success.

The world media would be looking over his shoulder, ready to jump at any chance to mock the effort or exploit it.

And all he could think about was an infuriating bundle of femininity and innocence who was slowly but irresistibly driving him nuts.

His narrowed eyes flicked to the computer console on the desk in front of him. The screen was filled with lines of words and symbols that had appeared in response to half a dozen keyboard strokes. He leaned forward slightly, studying them.

One in particular had caught his attention. Listed in the current issue of the *Journal of Antiquities* was "Correlations of Minoan and Aztec Pottery Motifs" by Dr. Cassia Jones of the Center for Advanced Studies.

With a few more keystrokes, he requested an electronic copy of the article. Moments later it flashed before him.

The brief author biography at the beginning of the article indicated that her particular area of expertise was linguistics. She was a world-recognized authority on languages, both ancient and modern, with credentials someone three times her age would have been proud to possess.

Tristan groaned inwardly, thinking of his response when Simon had introduced her as "Dr. Jones." He must have come across as the world's biggest chauvinist. No wonder she had swiftly absented herself.

As though that first impression hadn't been bad enough, he'd compounded the problem by failing to show the slightest interest in her work. Even after he learned of her association with the Center, he hadn't bothered to ask what sort of research projects she pursued.

The harm might already be done, but he was still driven to discover this part of her life. Once he began reading, he found himself quickly absorbed. This was a Cassia he didn't know: brilliant, insightful, logical.

Her complex data was clearly set forth, and her case built step-by-step to support the theory that explorers from Minoan Greece had influenced the pottery of the Aztec civilization in Mexico.

If she was correct, her findings had interesting ramifications for his own work.

He sat thinking about what he had read for a while, not simply the content but the way it was presented. More than ever he realized he had made a fundamental mistake with Cassia.

He had treated her as simply a beautiful woman, when in fact she possessed an intellect and imagination that at the very least rivaled his own.

A self-deprecating grin curved his mouth as he considered why he should have failed to realize what was now so obvious. The answer was hardly flattering, yet he could not elude it.

Somewhere deep inside he had sensed that, of all the people he had ever met, she was the only one who had a good chance of getting past his carefully constructed defenses to touch the vulnerable man within.

The mere possibility of that was highly threatening, so he had deliberately sabotaged his relationship with her before it could even get started.

With his customary ruthlessness, he admitted that he did not seem able to cope with her on a personal level. But that didn't mean they couldn't work together as professionals, especially when she obviously had a great deal to contribute to his current project.

The possibility that he was simply rationalizing his need to see her again did not elude him. Deciding that self-analysis shouldn't be allowed to go too far, he shrugged off that thought and reached for the phone.

Cassia was, as almost always, in her office. A high-ranking member of the government had requested an analysis of recent Soviet propaganda statements to determine if certain linguistic changes might indicate a shift in policy that could in turn open the way for negotiations.

As was the custom at the Center, when the request came in it was offered to whichever qualified member of the research staff wanted to pursue it. Cassia had volunteered, hoping that the challenge would distract her.

When the phone rang she ignored it, knowing Veda would answer. Moments later her concentration was shattered as the computer said, "Cassia, it's that man again."

The color washed from her cheeks, only to come rushing back more vividly than ever. An almost frightening wave of anticipation tightened the muscles of her stomach even as she realized that she had been subconsciously waiting and hoping for this moment for weeks. Strictly to buy time, she asked, "What man?"

Veda sighed. "Tristan Ward, the one you went out with but wouldn't tell me about. Remember, I went through my memory banks and did a report on him for you."

Cassia remembered. She had, reluctantly, read the report, in the process learning a great deal about Tristan's remarkable achievements but very little about him as a man. That wasn't Veda's fault; he was obviously an expert at revealing only that part of himself that he wanted known and no more.

"Oh . . . him. What does he want?"

"To talk with you. He says it's business."

The anticipation of a moment before plummeted into disappointment. Business. She should have known. Tristan had made it more than clear that he had no personal interest in her.

"Ask him to leave a message." Cowardly, but she just didn't feel up to coping with him at the moment. Later, when she'd had a chance to collect her thoughts, she'd call him back and . . .

"Well!" Veda exclaimed seconds later. "I've never been so insulted in my life. He says he isn't leaving any messages with 'a bunch of silicon chips.' Can you imagine him calling me such a thing?"

Cassia managed not to point out that the description was accurate, if incomplete. Veda didn't really seem all that miffed. If she had been, she would have hung up. "Oh, all right. I'll talk to him."

Moments later Tristan was on the line. "That computer is getting out of hand," he growled. "It thinks it's your mother."

After two months of doing her best to forget him, with absolutely no success, Cassia had hoped his first words would be somewhat more conciliatory. When that failed to be the case, she said coldly, "Veda is my business, not yours. What do you want?"

Tristan hesitated, taken aback by her tone. He hadn't meant to start off like that, but having to go through that damn machine had set his already strained nerves on edge. Cassia's attitude only made it worse. She sounded so . . . distant.

"I need to talk with you. Do you have some time this evening?"

She did, and she longed to see him, but she wasn't

about to admit any of that. "Possibly . . . What do we have to discuss?"

Smothering an impatient response, he forced himself to say quietly, "I've read that article you did on Minoan and Aztec pottery. You raised some interesting points that are related to some work I'm doing. I'd like us to . . . collaborate."

Such a dry, dusty word made Cassia instinctively rebellious. Her first impulse was to reject the suggestion out of hand, but she forced herself to think it over.

Whether she liked it or not, she did have certain responsibilities as a professional and a scholar. Pride would not permit her to forget herself. It simply would not do to let emotions get in the way of reason and logic.

"I suppose I could get free for a few minutes this evening."

Tristan had been unconsciously holding his breath while she thought things over. Now he released it in a soundless sigh. "Good. How about meeting me at the Oceanography Society around seven o'clock?"

Nonplussed by his choice, she found herself agreeing. "All right . . . where is that?"

Briskly, he gave her directions, confirmed the time, and hung up. Cassia was left staring at the phone, wondering if she had imagined the whole thing.

Veda finally roused her from her thoughts with a muted beep. When Cassia glanced in the direction of her electronic eye, the computer asked, "Shall I find out what Mr. Ward has to do with the Oceanography Society?"

Cassia nodded absently. "Yes . . . that might be a good idea." Seven o'clock. That left her about an hour to finish up what she was doing and change.

Not that there was anything wrong with the plain cotton skirt and blouse she wore. But after a day in the office they were a little wrinkled.

"I'll be upstairs," she told Veda as she left. Once in her apartment, she hurriedly showered and drew from the closet a sky blue knit dress she had never worn before.

Allegra had helped her pick it out on a recent shopping expedition Cassia suspected had been intended to cheer her up. The dress looked deceptively simple on its hanger, but once in place it hugged her curves unabashedly.

Staring at herself in the mirror, she frowned doubtfully. The dress might send the wrong signals.

She didn't want Tristan to think she was still interested in him in any but the most professional way, even though the opposite did happen to be the case.

"You look very nice," Veda commented. After Cassia had left the office, the computer had routinely switched off her monitor down there and transferred her activities to the apartment.

Along the way she had also completed her most recent check of the data banks for any new information on Tristan Ward.

"I found out why Mr. Ward is familiar with the

Oceanography Society. He's been a member there for some years and spoke at a luncheon just last month about something called the *Questor* project. It was routinely noted in the minutes of the organization, but no details were given."

"Is that usual?" Cassia asked as she ran a brush through her hair.

"No, as a matter of fact it seems quite out of the ordinary. My guess is that he chose to speak off the record."

"I wonder why. What could Questor be that would require such confidentiality?"

"Perhaps you will learn that tonight."

Cassia hoped so. Tristan represented enough mysteries without adding one more. After assuring Veda that she would not be late, she picked up her purse and headed out the door.

Downstairs in the lobby of the Center, she waved to the guard but did not stop. Since the night of Allegra and Simon's party, she had not made use of any of the staff drivers.

Fred had recovered completely from the altercation, except for his pride, but continued to give her a wide berth. One of the administrators had suggested she use a different chauffeur, and had been surprised by her refusal to do so.

Several memos had come her way politely pointing out that the limousine service existed for the convenience of the staff. She had ignored them, but did not kid herself that the matter would be dropped.

Her rebellion against the constraints of her world

was bound to be noted. Sooner or later, an effort would be made to bring her back into line.

On this warm spring night, it was pleasant to stroll along the city streets, part of the perpetual throng heading who knew where.

While she was not so naive as to wander into less well-lit and -populated areas, she felt perfectly safe walking south along Fifth Avenue toward the white marble building that housed the Oceanography Society.

A remnant of a more gracious age, the Society's headquarters might have been another of the exclusive clubs that nestled along the side streets of midtown. In fact, it had once been little more than that, back when scientific exploration was the preserve of the wealthy and leisured.

These days membership in the Society was awarded strictly by achievement, not position. Yet a certain old-world sense of privilege still lingered in the hushed atmosphere of a reception hall furnished with choice antiques and paintings that would have been welcomed by the most discerning museum.

A quick glance around told Cassia that she was the only woman on view, and that her arrival had prompted a very discreet but still unmistakable stir.

Bespectacled gentlemen glanced up from their reading to stare at her. Several coughed, and a few of the older ones cocked their heads together and muttered.

From behind a mahogany desk, a uniformed employee approached her. He was an elderly man somewhere between seventy and one hundred who looked as though he had not changed a whit since the day the Society first opened its doors almost a century before.

His voice was low and carried a hint of skepticism, as though he had already decided she was an interloper who had wandered in off the street and needed to be directed back there posthaste. "May I . . . uh . . . assist you, madame?"

Cassia hid a smile and nodded politely. "I'm Dr. Jones. I believe Mr. Ward is expecting me."

This took a moment to register. When it did, the gentleman inclined his head gravely, as though in acceptance of the remorselessness of change battering down the last strongholds of tradition, and gravely indicated that she should proceed to the bar where, he informed her, Mr. Ward awaited.

So he did. Tristan was seated in a booth toward the back, facing the door. He had apparently been keeping an eye out for her, since he spotted her immediately and rose.

As she walked toward him, Cassia was more aware than she would have liked to be of the looks she was getting from the other men. They ran the gamut from the mildly curious to the unabashedly interested.

It occurred to her to wonder if she had always received such attention, and if so, why she was only noticing it now. The explanation wasn't hard to come by. Tristan made her acutely conscious of herself as a woman, and of all that implied.

As he stepped away from the table to meet her, she noted a certain protectiveness in his attitude. His eyes ran over her appreciatively in a way that was not really all that different from the other men's, yet did not spark the same reaction.

Instead of feeling vaguely embarrassed and threatened, she was pleased by his obvious approval, even though she did her best to hide it. When his hand lightly touched her arm, she frowned and sat down quickly.

Tristan resumed his seat across from her, but not before shooting a glance at the other men that caused their attention to be abruptly refocused elsewhere.

He regarded her quietly as he said, "I'm glad you could make it on such short notice."

Cassia shrugged, relieved that he couldn't see her hands twisting in her lap. She was half pleased, half dismayed that he didn't seem to have changed at all in the last two months, except that he looked more tired.

Certainly the effect he had on her was still the same. In an effort to deny it, she said, "I felt like getting out anyway."

His mouth tightened slightly as the suggestion that she didn't particularly care who she was with hit home. The waiter arrived at that moment, preventing whatever response he might have made.

When they had given their orders and were once again alone, Tristan asked, "How's everything at the Center?"

"About the same. How's your work going?"

"Fine . . . I guess. There's a new project about to get underway."

Cassia nodded her thanks to the waiter as he set a glass of white wine in front of her. She took a sip before she asked, "Is that Questor?"

Tristan's eyebrows rose fractionally. "How did you know about that?"

"Veda found a mention of it in the Society's journal."

He relaxed slightly and shot her a pleased smile. "At your request, I suppose?"

"No," Cassia informed him blandly, "it was on her own initiative. Veda . . . takes a lot on herself."

He swallowed his disappointment along with his beer. "I've noticed that. Was it your intention when you designed her?"

"Not exactly, although I should have anticipated it. Veda is supposed to be able to benefit from her experiences—in effect, to learn. I guess one of the things she's learned is to be independent and think for herself."

"Always a good philosophy, but I have to admit it's a little disconcerting in a machine."

And in a woman? Cassia caught herself wondering if that was why he had never asked her out again; did he find her too assertive and unfeminine, whatever that meant?

It hurt to think so, but she told herself it didn't matter. She was who she was.

What changes she wanted to see happen in her life did not include a complete alteration of her personality to fit some man's notions of how a woman should be.

In an effort to turn the conversation into safer

channels, she said, "You mentioned something about my article on Minoan and Aztec pottery. . . ."

Tristan nodded reluctantly. He had all but forgotten his resolve to stick strictly to business. "Yes. I found it very interesting. It seems to support an idea of mine regarding the legend of Atlantis."

Cassia's eyes widened slightly. Of all the topics she might have expected him to be interested in, Atlantis wasn't one of them. It fell into the murky area of myth and fantasy exploited by pseudoscientists out to bilk a gullible public.

"Atlantis . . . ?" she murmured at last. "That's just a legend created by Plato as an example of what he considered to be an ideal society."

"No one knows that for sure," Tristan countered. "We say that's the case because there's no civilization—and for that matter, no land—in the place where he said Atlantis existed. So we conclude it was all a fantasy. But just because it isn't there now doesn't mean it never was."

"But . . . an entire culture of the complexity Plato described couldn't just vanish without a trace."

"Of course not. There are traces. For example, traditional Minoan designs showing up three thousand years later on Aztec pottery. Your article demonstrated pretty conclusively that the designs are too similar to be coincidence. So how did they get from one side of the world to the other and, just as importantly, how were they preserved for so long?"

Cassia shook her head in bewilderment. "I have

no idea. All I did was correlate my observations and draw the obvious conclusions."

"Exactly what I've done over and over when I've encountered similar cases. There are more of them than you might expect, all pointing to trade between the ancient Greeks and the Aztecs' forebears."

"I suppose that's possible," she conceded, "judging from what I've read about prevailing ocean currents and so on. But with the immense distances involved I can't believe contact could have been very frequent."

"Not unless there was someone in the middle, another culture between the two, where ships from both the Mediterranean region and the Americas could meet and transfer cargoes. In other words, Atlantis."

"If you're right," Cassia eventually said after she had mulled over his argument, "then what happened to it? How did it vanish without a trace?"

"I don't know," Tristan admitted. "But I intend to find out. With *Questor.*"

"I have a feeling I'm going to regret this, but what is Questor?"

He leaned forward, his eyes alight with an inner vision. "The most technologically sophisticated ocean-going research vessel ever built. It took the better part of a decade to design, and no expense has been spared in its construction. If Atlantis does exist, it's going to lead us there."

There was no boastfulness in that simple statement. Tristan clearly meant it. His enthusiasm and his faith were unmistakable.

But then, why shouldn't they be? He was a man accustomed to achieving whatever he set out to do.

It was the eagerness she felt in him that impressed Cassia the most. How long had it been since she had experienced such wholehearted commitment to a project? Her work, important as it was, seemed boring in comparison.

She couldn't help but envy him the possession of so daring and romantic a dream. Nor could she resist the urge to share it with him.

Their gazes met across the table. The drone of voices around them died away. They were alone on a tiny island of their own making, cut off from everyone and everything else.

Without touching, without saying a word, they spoke to each other with the voices of heart and mind.

In an instant, Cassia knew what he was about to ask her . . . and how she would respond.

Chapter 5

"Why," Veda asked somewhat plaintively, "are you doing this?"

"I've already explained that to you," Cassia said patiently. "Because I'm excited about the project. I think it's very worthwhile."

She went on packing as she spoke. The suitcase was almost filled with shorts, shirts, bathing suits, and a few dresses, but she thought she could fit a couple more things in. After all, there was no telling how long she would be gone.

The white jeans and T-shirt she wore were typical of the wardrobe she was taking with her. Anything that wasn't casual, comfortable, and easy to care for was being left behind.

Where she was going, there would be little time or energy to expend on her appearance.

In preparation for the trip, she had taken her courage in her hands and gone to Allegra's beauty salon to request a trouble-free style. When she walked out several hours later, it was with something of a feeling of shock.

Her waist-length hair had been ruthlessly cut to little more than a cap of feathery curls clinging to her well-shaped head. The style emphasized the delicate purity of her features and made her blue-gray eyes look larger than ever.

She was, though she did not realize it, lovelier than at any previous time in her life.

Yet she also carried a hint of sadness, and more than a touch of aching vulnerability that seemed to mirror her doubts about what she was doing.

"Everyone here says it's crazy," Veda pointed out, rather unnecessarily.

Cassia had been getting notes to that effect ever since announcing her decision four days before to participate in "Project *Questor*."

Reaction ranged from disbelief to outright disparagement. But all were unanimous that she was nuts to have anything to do with the venture.

When one of the directors had finally taken it upon himself to discuss the matter with her directly, he had rather nervously pointed out, "Dr. Jones, your services here have always been greatly appreciated, but lately we have noted a, shall we say, change in attitude that is most distressing."

Cassia hadn't disagreed with him. She knew that she was no longer the absentminded scholar she had once been, amenable to having all her decisions made for her and asking for nothing except a quiet place to work.

If she hadn't met Tristan, her discontentment would most likely have taken longer to emerge, but eventually it would have become obvious. Though he was not the cause of her decision to make fundamental changes in her life, he was certainly a catalyst.

Never again would she be able to think of the world, and of herself, in dispassionate terms. All the long suppressed sensuality of her nature was finally coming to the fore, and bringing with it an overwhelming need for freedom.

"If you mean I've stopped letting my life be arranged for me," she had told the director quietly, "you're right. I will always value my years at the Center, and I would certainly like to remain associated with it, but it's time I considered other things as well."

The plump, smooth-faced man had shaken his head in bewilderment. "I don't understand. We have always done our utmost to see that you had everything you needed. Peace and quiet for your work, no distractions, generous financial support. What more could you possibly want?"

He was so obviously sincere that Cassia had felt no anger toward him. Only a bit of wistfulness at the ending of one part of her life, greatly overshadowed by her excitement at what lay ahead.

"I have no complaint with the Center," she had said gently, "except that I've outgrown it. This is a . . . hothouse . . . only instead of plants you have people. You nurture our intellects, encourage our curiosity, pamper and indulge us. But all the while we're kept apart from the real world. I just don't want to live like that anymore."

"I can understand, just barely, why you might feel too restricted here," the director had conceded. "But is this *Questor* business the answer? That's hardly part of the real world."

"It's what I want the real world to be," Cassia had explained gently. "A place where people can dare to dream."

She had known even as she spoke that she wasn't getting through to him. Though they were far too polite to say so, he and the other directors saw her as a rebellious child.

Her aspirations were so illogical to them that they had even graciously offered to keep her post open, making it clear in doing so that they believed she would be back in no time flat.

Cassia had other plans. Though she had no intention of severing her connection with the Center entirely—she was, for example, continuing her work with Veda—she never again intended to be locked away in a prison of the mind. There was too much more to life.

Veda, however, saw things differently. She made it clear that to her the Center was the world.

To go beyond it demanded a leap of faith she could not yet manage. But neither could she accept the idea of being separated from Cassia.

The solution lay in the peculiar nature of computers. The physical reality of Veda—her main memory banks and circuit boards so complex as to require constant levels of temperature and humidity—was staying right where it had always been in a sealed room adjoining Cassia's office.

But a portable module was leaving with her, taking the eyes and ears and voice of Veda into the world.

It remained to be seen where Veda would consider herself to be—still in the little room, or on board *Questor*—or in both places at the same time.

The answer to that puzzle would tell Cassia something about a subject she already suspected humans would never know the full truth of how artificial intelligence conceived a sense of self.

But for the moment, she had her own self to get in hand.

Having accepted Tristan's invitation to join *Questor*, she knew there was no possibility of going back on her word. That did not, however, prevent her from being assailed by doubts.

Not about the search itself. She matter-of-factly accepted that it was, at best, a long shot.

Looking at the facts objectively, she was at a loss to explain Tristan's confident assurance that they would find Atlantis. Nothing he had told her held out more than a remote possibility of that.

Yet the venture was still worth pursuing. Scientists frequently followed vague hints and blurred trails to make their most exciting discoveries. Intuition—whatever that meant—played an important part in any major breakthrough.

It wasn't *Questor* itself that worried her. At worst,

she could look forward to several weeks of interesting work. It was the proximity to Tristan that gave her pause.

His abrupt disappearance two months before had made her feel all the pain of rejection for the first time in her life.

Much as she had tried not to, she had spent hours wondering what it was about her that had made him decide not to see her again.

If she hadn't been so attracted to him, it wouldn't have mattered. But as it was, she couldn't deny that his opinion counted a great deal with her.

She wanted him to like and respect her. Even more, she needed him to recognize the passion he had unleashed in her and return it fully.

That was, she felt sure, a fruitless wish. Tristan had made it clear he did not desire her. He saw her simply as a skilled professional who could make a contribution to his project.

The challenge, for her, would be to accept him on that level alone while not yearning for more than he was willing to give.

Having done a final check to be sure she wasn't forgetting anything, Cassia closed her suitcase and lugged it over to the door. Then she turned to Veda.

Quietly, in a tone one might use to a child about to embark on a frightening adventure, she said, "It's time to pack your monitor. The one in my office will be left on, and of course all your main circuits will be functioning."

"But I won't be able to communicate with you until we reach wherever we're going," Veda murmured. Since learning of Cassia's plans, she had voiced the same complaint several times despite all efforts to reassure her.

"Don't be concerned about that," Cassia soothed patiently. "Everything will be fine. When I hook you up again, we'll be on board *Questor.*"

Before Veda could comment further, Cassia turned off the monitor and swiftly disassembled it. Within half an hour the various parts were neatly packed in a carrying case.

She took a last glance around the apartment before hoisting the case over her shoulder. It weighed less than twenty pounds, so she could carry it comfortably.

The rest of her luggage would be sent through, but Veda would remain with her throughout the trip.

The flight to Grand Bahama Island was uneventful. Cassia spent the time going over the information Tristan had provided about *Questor.*

As she studied a schematic drawing of the ship and read about its remarkable abilities, she couldn't help but be impressed by the imagination and intelligence of its design.

Tristan had not only brought together the latest state-of-the-art technology in navigation, undersea exploration, and so on, but he had also designed several important innovations that would enable the searchers to stay below the surface longer and cover more territory.

Every inch of the eighty-foot vessel served a purpose. Nothing was wasted, and all the parts fit together perfectly to form an efficient, and rather beautiful whole.

Questor was a glimpse into a part of Tristan that Cassia had not encountered before. Instead of the superficial, often hard sophistication she had seen in him, she now recognized brilliant creativity and a restless curiosity that matched her own.

By the time she had landed at Grand Bahama Island and made her way to the check-in desk of the small airline that would take her on the final leg of her journey, she was more aware than ever of how greatly he attracted her, and how careful she would have to be not to think of him in anything but the most impersonal terms.

Even this early in the summer, the weather was already hot and sultry. Cassia was content to sit quietly for the few minutes until her flight was called.

As the small eight-seater plane took off, she gazed down at the waving palm trees, white sand beaches, and verdant hills dotted with vibrant tropical flowers.

For a brief moment, she felt a stab of longing to share all the beauty and tranquillity with someone she truly cared about.

Well aware of exactly who she had in mind, Cassia pushed the thought aside. She was there to do a job, nothing more, and would be wise to keep her thoughts strictly on business.

Almost before she realized it, the plane began its descent toward her destination, the southernmost of

the Bimini Islands. From the airport it was a short
taxi ride to the harbor where *Questor* was docked.

On the way, Cassia drank in the cheerful sights,
sounds, and scents of the island.

Spirited reggae tunes flowed from the doorways of
pastel-hued buildings. Brightly dressed men and
women clustered in the narrow streets, selling their
wares in the fast patter of the island patois. Delectable aromas of curried chicken, fresh mangos, and
flowering bougainvillea and jacaranda bushes per-
fumed the air.

She was just wishing that she had come a few days
earlier to spend some time getting to know the place
when the taxi pulled up to a dock and all thoughts of
anything but the project itself vanished from her
mind.

Questor lay at rest, her pristine white bow rising
and falling gently with the sea swell. Her vast decks
were crowded with equipment, but everything was
neatly stowed, giving the impression of meticulous
order and purpose.

Near her prow was the deep-sea submersible in
which scientists could safely remain for hours as they
examined the ocean bottom. Close by was a large
microwave dish that would link the ship to the
outside world.

A small cabin on the deck served as a temporary
laboratory where any artifacts that were found
would be immediately treated for preservation before being transported to the larger labs below deck.

From the roof of the pilothouse, other antennae
rose into the sky. Cassia knew the ship boasted the

latest in navigation and communication equipment, but actually seeing the evidence of that in the flesh—so to speak—brought home to her the full extent of Tristan's commitment to the project.

He had spared no effort or expense to make sure that his search would have every possible chance of succeeding.

The taxi driver unloaded her luggage, accepted his payment, including a generous tip, and took himself off. Cassia glanced from the pile of bags to the ramp leading from dock to deck and back again.

She sighed ruefully. Four or five trips would be needed to get everything on board.

Adjusting the shoulder bag holding Veda, she picked up the first suitcase and started forward. Before she had gotten more than a few steps, a deep voice undercut by humor instructed her to stop right where she was.

"Hold it! Just what do you think you're doing, sweetheart? Trying to wreck the reputation of every man aboard *Questor?*"

Bounding out of the midship cabin and down the ramp came a young man in his early twenties wearing cutoff jeans, a smile, and nothing else.

Tall, tanned, and tousled-haired, he looked as though he should be on a California beach with a surfboard under one arm and a curvaceous girlfriend under the other, instead of on a research vessel.

His eyes wandered over her appreciatively as he said, "Hi, gorgeous. I'm Hank Davies, at your service. Forget about whatever stuffy old yacht you're looking for and come on board."

His exuberance was such that she couldn't help but smile. "Actually, Mr. Davies, I think I've found the right place. This is *Questor*, isn't it?"

He looked puzzled, but nodded. "That's us. But how did we get so lucky? I figured you for one of the yachting crowd."

Smiling to take any sting out of her words, she said, "You figured wrong. I'm Cassia Jones, crew member. Do you think I could get some help with my gear?"

Hank's response was as comical as it was unfeigned. His mouth dropped open as he stared at her in blank amazement. "You're Dr. Jones? The hotshot genius from that New York think tank?"

Cassia's mouth quirked, but she restrained an impulse to laugh. "That's not exactly how I'd describe myself, but it'll do."

"Tristan told us you were coming, but he said . . ." Hank broke off, apparently struggling to reconcile whatever he had been told with the lovely vision before him.

Unable to restrain her curiosity, Cassia prompted, " . . . He said . . ."

"Uh . . . just that you were really brilliant and we were lucky to get you and we shouldn't . . ." He broke off, flushing.

"Shouldn't what?"

Hank hesitated before he said, "I just got the impression that you were one of those eggheads who walks around in a fog all the time." He grinned broadly. "But now I realize ol' Tristan had another reason for telling us to steer clear. No offense, ma'am, but you're about the best lookin' woman I've ever seen."

Cassia was hardly offended by so sincere a compliment, but she was at a loss as to how to respond. She wasn't about to be rude to Hank, yet neither did she want to give him the wrong impression about her availability.

Settling on a simple "thank you," she picked up one of her bags and started toward the ramp. "I'd better get on board. We're due to sail soon, aren't we?"

With a rueful smile, he hoisted the rest of her luggage as easily as if it were weightless and trotted after her, not unlike a very large, very friendly puppy. "The boss runs a tight ship. I expect we'll be leaving right on time."

"You wouldn't happen to know which cabin I've been assigned?" she asked when they reached the deck.

"As a matter of fact, I do. You're right next to the lab. Ought to be convenient for you once we start bringing stuff up."

"How soon do you think that will be?"

Hank shrugged and started down a short flight of steps that led into the narrow gangway. He glanced over his shoulder at Cassia as she followed. "It's hard to say. The boss seems to have a pretty fair idea of where he wants to look. If he's right and we get lucky, we should be able to keep you busy real soon. Otherwise, who knows?"

"What's your part in all this?" Cassia asked as they arrived at her cabin. It was on the port side near the bow. To the left was the entrance to the lab. To the right was an unmarked door.

"I'm one of the divers," Hank told her proudly as he set her luggage down. Her suitcases alone took up most of the tiny but well-furnished space.

A pull-down bunk hung from one wall with built-in cabinets behind it for clothes and personal belongings. Opposite that was a desk with bookshelves above and drawers beneath. A separate area, about the size of a small closet, held the commode, sink, and shower.

"Believe it or not," Hank said, "this is plush accommodation for *Questor.* Just about every inch of space is taken up by equipment."

"I hope I haven't put anyone out," Cassia murmured, glancing around dubiously. It didn't make sense that on such a carefully planned voyage the cabin would have been left empty.

Hank laughed. "Just the boss. He's bunking in his office. Guess he figured a lady needed a few comforts."

Cassia smothered a groan. The last person she wanted to be in debt to was Tristan. "That's ridiculous," she said firmly. "He can have his cabin back. I'll just make do like everyone else."

Her newfound friend grinned. "Good idea. All the rest of us are doubling up. Maybe we could draw straws to see who gets to share with you."

"Uh . . . on second thought . . ."

Some of Hank's good-natured youthfulness fled as he looked down at her challengingly. He was standing only a few feet away, his bare chest gleaming and his powerful legs planted slightly apart.

The smallness of the cabin, coupled with his nearness and the appreciative gleam in his eyes, suddenly made Cassia nervous.

She backed away slightly as he asked softly, "You don't want ol' Tristan thinkin' you need special handling, do you?"

"I don't especially care what he thinks," Cassia claimed, wishing she meant it. Hank apparently decided she did, for his smile widened as he took another step toward her.

"I'm sure glad to hear that, ma'am. It'd be an awful shame if you were already spoken for."

The laughter was gone from his eyes. In its place was a virile hunger that made Cassia curse her naiveté. She had suspected right from the start that she might be giving Hank the wrong impression, but hadn't known how to prevent it.

Now it looked as though she should have tried harder. Ruefully, she concluded that he apparently had a thing for older women.

With her back literally against the wall, she struggled for something to say that would discourage him without hurting his feelings. "I think you've got the wrong idea. I'm here strictly to work."

He shrugged that off good-naturedly. "It's going to be a long voyage."

"That doesn't matter." More firmly, she added, "Thank you for helping with my bags. Now, if you'll excuse me, I'd like to unpack."

"Later. Let's get better acquainted first." The small distance remaining between them shrank alarmingly as he suddenly reached out a hand and, as though drawn by an irresistible impulse, touched the soft feathers of her hair with surprising gentleness.

The tough-guy pose eroded slightly as he murmured, "You can't blame a guy for wanting to get to know you better. Who wouldn't?"

Plenty of men, she suspected, who were a little older or wiser than Hank and would have caught even the inept signals she sent out.

For all his beachboy good looks and superficial sophistication, she suspected he wasn't much more experienced than she was herself.

Gently, she said, "Hank, we have to work together, remember. It's just good policy not to muck that up."

He hesitated, belatedly aware that he might be in over his head and willing to accept a graceful way out. "Do you really mean that? You can't mix business and . . . uh . . . pleasure?"

"I do," Cassia assured him gravely. "It would just be too distracting."

Flattered at the implied suggestion that he would sweep her off her feet and make it impossible for her to concentrate, Hank grinned. His hand dropped away from her as he took a step back. "I guess I see what you mean. No hard feelings?"

Having assured him that there were none, Cassia watched in relief as he prepared to leave. She liked Hank and was sure they would get along, but she hoped he would spread the word that she was unavailable for extracurricular activities.

Standing at the open door of the cabin, she exchanged a few last words with him. He looked down at her a bit sheepishly as he said, "Thanks for not getting mad at me, Cassia. I know I came on too strong."

Touched by his apology, she smiled gently. "That's okay, Hank. If I were five years younger and not so caught up in my work, I've no doubt you would have had better luck."

He laughed, clearly suspecting she was being kind but willing enough to accept that. In a surprisingly courtly gesture, he took one of her hands in his and pressed a gentle kiss to the tips of her fingers. "I think *Questor* is lucky to have you, ma'am. You're some kind of lady."

Cassia was still blushing at his praise as he took himself off down the gangway. She stood for a moment looking after him bemusedly until a sardonic voice abruptly drew her up short.

"How touching. You can't have been on board ten minutes and already you're making idiots of my crew."

Whirling, Cassia found Tristan standing in the open doorway of the cabin to the right of her own, his expression a daunting mixture of anger and contempt that changed to one of amazement as he took in her appearance.

"What the hell have you done to yourself?" he demanded. "Especially your hair. It's . . . not there anymore."

"I got it cut," Cassia snapped, struggling to ignore the stab of hurt his obvious disapproval provoked.

Telling herself she didn't give a tinker's damn what he thought of her appearance, she demanded, "Just who do you think you are, going at me like that about Hank? You know perfectly well I haven't done anything wrong."

"Do I?" Tristan shot back. Her new hairstyle emphasized her delicate beauty to such an extent that just looking at her made him even more vividly aware of the treacherous attraction he felt for her. He was damned if he would let her know what she did to him.

"That kid acted like he didn't know what the hell had hit him." He sneered derisively. "For God's sake, he's only twenty-two years old. Don't you think you ought to pick on someone a little dryer behind the ears?"

"I'll have you know I did nothing except agree to let him carry my luggage." Stung, she added, "At least he was kind enough to meet me when I arrived, unlike certain other people I could mention."

"I was busy," Tristan insisted defensively, all too well aware that he had deliberately found out when she was likely to show up and arranged to be busy below decks just so he wouldn't look as though he had been waiting around for her.

Now he regretted the childishness of that, but had no idea how to make up for it. Instead, he claimed loftily, "Some of us have work to do."

"Oh, pardon me!" Cassia exclaimed. She was in no mood to let that go by without an appropriate rejoinder. "You couldn't be disturbed for two seconds to say hello, but you can lurk around in hallways waiting to cast aspersions on perfectly innocent people's characters."

Tristan glared at her. "Innocent? You could have given Mata Hari lessons. I doubt Hank can remember what his name is. And furthermore, I do not lurk!"

"Hank may be a whole lot younger than you," Cassia taunted, deliberately twisting Tristan's reference to the diver's youthfulness, "but he has tons more sense. Enough to know when to back off."

His green eyes turned hard, like glinting bits of emerald shot through with light. "Are you saying I don't? Maybe you need to be reminded of whose ship this is. I can damn well do what I please."

The sheer audacity of that took Cassia's breath away, but only for a moment. "Says who? You hired me to interpret your findings, not to put up with your insults. I've got a good mind to go straight back to New York!"

"Go ahead! Run back to your ivory tower. It'd be just like you to chicken out the first time you try to face the real world!"

Cassia opened her mouth to reply in kind, only to abruptly clamp it shut again. Insufferable bully! She absolutely was not going to sink to his level.

Drawing herself to her full height, which still left her considerably short of his six feet plus, she said stiffly, "If you think for one moment that you can provoke me into leaving, forget it. You're obviously having regrets about asking me to join this expedi-

tion, but that's just too bad. I came to do a job, and
I'm staying until it's finished."

Immensely relieved that she wasn't going to take
him up on his challenge to go, Tristan still managed
to glower at her. "Just stay away from my crew," he
ordered. "The next few weeks are going to be tough
enough without some wide-eyed blonde deciding to
test her wiles on them!"

Cassia stared at him, stupified. It had never occurred to her that she possessed such a thing as
wiles. They were the province of women far different
from herself.

Yet Tristan seemed convinced she was some lethal
femme fatale from whom no man was safe. Trying
hard to muster anger at that attitude, she had to fight
down a sneaking sense of pleasure.

So he thought she could make idiots out of men
and lead his crew astray? She bit back a giggle at the
thought of herself as some ancient siren drawing
unwary men onto the shoals of heartbreak.

That was just plain silly. It didn't take any great
brilliance to see that it was really himself he feared
for.

The long weeks ahead, when they would be
thrown together repeatedly within the narrow confines of *Questor*'s world, suddenly seemed very
promising indeed.

Tristan's venture into the unknown might not turn
up anything, but she suspected hers just might turn
out better than she had dared to hope.

Chapter 6

"So this is *Questor*," Veda sniffed. "Big deal."

Cassia laughed softly. She had barely hooked the monitor up, connecting it through the microwave transmitter to the computer back at the Center, when Veda had begun making her opinions clear. Nothing met with her approval, let alone impressed her.

It was a relief to know that she had survived their brief separation with her spirit undiminished.

"Just how seaworthy is this bucket of bolts?" Veda inquired skeptically. "I don't think I can swim."

"I don't think you remember your manners," Cassia gently rebuked. "We're very privileged to be here. There's never been an expedition like this before, or a ship like *Questor*."

"Easy to see why," Veda muttered.

"Grouch. You're going to be so busy here you won't have time to worry."

"Busy doing what? All I see so far is a fair-to-middling laboratory with some pretty decent equipment but nothing to analyze."

"That will change," Cassia assured her with rather more confidence than she really felt. "As soon as the divers start bringing artifacts to the surface, we'll be swamped."

"I won't hold my breath."

"You don't have any breath . . . Oh, what's the use? You'll complain no matter what I say." Eyeing the little computer, Cassia asked, "You aren't . . . homesick, are you?"

"Homesick?" Veda repeated pensively. "That means 'a longing for home and family while absent from them.' No, I don't think I'm homesick. After all, you're here."

"Then how do you feel?"

There was silence for a moment before Veda said softly, "Do you realize that's the first time you've asked me that?"

Cassia nodded gravely. Somehow it had never seemed right before. Now it did. "I guess I'm just beginning to admit to myself that you do have feelings."

"They're a rather mixed blessing," Veda pointed out dryly.

"I'll say! We humans have been trying to figure out how to cope with them for millennia."

"Any tips you can give me?"

Cassia thought that over before she said quietly, "Only to be true to yourself. You can't spend your life fulfilling other people's expectations."

It didn't occur to her that this was an odd way to be talking to a machine. On the contrary. What she had just said applied equally to both Veda and herself.

For how many years now had she lived according to a plan laid out by others? All her life, really.

At first being set on a course that suited her special abilities had been a blessing. But after a while, she had begun to realize something was missing. She couldn't just follow a road laid down by others, not when the world offered so much more.

In many ways, Tristan had had a far rougher time of it than she had. But in one way he was very fortunate; he had been compelled from the earliest age to find his own path. Meeting him, getting to know him even slightly, had confirmed Cassia's growing belief that it was time for her to do the same.

Leaving Veda to mull over the thorny problem of personal identity, she headed up on deck. Most of the crew was already there, watching as they cast off. She caught a glimpse of Tristan in the pilothouse, his face intent as he began carefully maneuvering *Questor* away from the dock.

As the ship's powerful engines surged to life beneath her, she felt a heady sense of exhilaration. The daring search for an elusive dream was at last beginning, and she was truly part of it.

The rest of the crew clearly felt the same way.

Whatever qualms they might have felt about being joined by a young, attractive woman, they put them aside to welcome her to the venture.

Even before the Biminis had faded behind them, Cassia was feeling very much at home. Enough so that when Tristan called them all up to the pilot-house to discuss the first stage of the expedition, she could face him without a qualm.

The hard stare he shot at her as she arrived with Hank and several of the other divers prompted only a sweet smile. She took her place at the large conference table well aware that he was still angry with her, but determined not to let that dim her pleasure in the moment.

Tristan waited until they had all settled down before addressing the dozen people regarding him with mingled eagerness and curiosity. He deliberately avoided looking at Cassia as he said, "First, I want you all to know that each of you signed on for this trip without receiving much information about where we'd be going and what we could expect to find. I appreciate your willingness to act on faith, and I hope you'll agree with me that it was worthwhile."

He let that sink in, then went on, "Now that we've sailed, security precautions that were necessary when we were still tied to land can be eased. I'm sure you've all got questions, so fire away."

There was a moment's silence before one of the senior members of the crew, Dr. Jason Lombard, a marine archaeologist, took the floor. He was an older man of about sixty with weathered features, thick silvery hair, and a lean, tough body that bespoke a life of hard work.

Cassia knew him by reputation as the highly respected discoverer of underwater archaeological remains in the Mediterranean. His presence on board *Questor* went a long way toward asserting the expedition's seriousness.

"Suppose we begin," he said quietly, "by hearing what it is you've got up your sleeve."

At Tristan's startled look, Dr. Lombard chuckled and went on good-humoredly. "There's no sense pretending you don't know what I mean. It's been obvious from the start that you knew more than you were telling."

"I didn't realize I was that transparent," Tristan murmured wryly.

The men laughed. It was clear to Cassia that they all held him in great respect, but that didn't mean they didn't enjoy teasing him just a bit.

"You always did play your cards close to the chest," Sean Garrison pointed out.

The head of the diving team was a well-built man in his early forties with thinning gray-blond hair and impenetrable black eyes that seemed to have seen everything at least once. "I ought to know, having sat across a poker table from you more than once!"

"But this time," Tristan said softly, "I wasn't bluffing." He stood up and opened a drawer of a nearby metal cabinet. From it he took a leather folder that he placed on the table before him and carefully opened.

Cassia was sitting too far away to see what was

inside, but she did not miss his intentness as he said, "It must have occurred to you all that I was launching this expedition on damned little evidence. For one reason or another, you were too polite to mention that, but I'm sure you had more than a few doubts."

The men glanced at one another abashedly, then back at him. "It's time for me to share with you the true basis of *Questor*'s search," Tristan said quietly, "and the reason I'm so confident we will succeed."

Without further explanation, he turned the folder around and slid it to the center of the table. Cassia leaned forward eagerly along with the rest.

She saw a frayed piece of yellowish opaque material about six inches wide and eight inches long that was slightly warped, as though it had once been kept rolled. Across it in a neat series of lines were inscribed a series of symbols.

It took her only a moment to flip through her mental filing cards and recognize the material as papyrus and the symbols as hieroglyphics from the Old Kingdom of Egypt, approximately forty-five hundred years old.

Several of the men around the table, including Dr. Lombard, had also recognized the source, if not perhaps the probable age of the document, but all were puzzled by it.

Their gazes shifted to her as Tristan said, "Dr. Jones is our resident expert on linguistics. Care to tell us what you make of this?"

Cassia sighed inwardly. She recognized the offer

for what it was: a challenge. Fortunately, she was more than up to it.

After studying the papyrus more closely, she said, "This appears to be a letter sent from a royal envoy back to the Pharaoh's court reporting on a journey undertaken for the Pharaoh. The grammar and vocabulary indicate the letter dates from the fourth dynasty of the Old Kingdom, or approximately the same time that the great pyramids were being built."

She continued her careful reading, going slowly to make the clearest possible interpretation. "Reference is made to difficulties encountered during the voyage and . . . sacrifices made to the gods upon the envoy's safe arrival at what he calls the . . . 'western isle.' He seems to give a fairly detailed explanation of how he reached the isle . . . including actual directions."

This last part was said on a rising note of enthusiasm as she recognized the full import of what lay before her. If—and it still remained highly speculative—if the "western isle" was Atlantis, the papyrus might in effect amount to a map pointing the way to it.

Her eyes were glowing and her cheeks slightly flushed as she looked up to find Tristan studying her intently. His gaze was admiring, and something more.

Something far more primitive flickered deep within his eyes before he said, "Not bad for a spontaneous translation. I'll save you some trouble and tell you that the papyrus has been completely interpreted—and authenticated—by Professor Abdul al-Bardi at Cairo University."

Cassia couldn't help but be impressed, and gratified that her own translation was supported by so eminent a scholar. Al-Bardi was one of the most highly respected Egyptologists in the world.

She could well understand why Tristan had taken the papyrus to him. What didn't make sense was why, once he had grasped its significance, the professor hadn't joined the expedition.

Tentatively, she asked, "Am I correct in thinking that Professor al-Bardi suffered a heart attack a few months ago?"

Tristan nodded. "He did, and his recovery is proving more difficult than he had hoped. I left his slot on the expedition open as long as possible, so long, in fact, that for a while it looked as though we might have to go without a linguist."

Until he had stumbled across her article and realized how useful she could be to him. Glumly, Cassia wondered if she had misunderstood his earlier anger when he found her with Hank. Perhaps he really did want her only for the professional expertise she could provide.

If that were the case, she was determined to find out. Uncertainty might lend a certain spice to life, but it could also get rather tedious. She wanted some indication from Tristan of his true feelings, and she meant to have it posthaste.

As it turned out, the papyrus offered her just the opening she needed. "If you wouldn't mind," she began, "I would like to study this in more detail."

"Of course," Tristan agreed readily, bemused by the sudden flare of determination he saw in her eyes. "Why don't you take it along to the lab and I'll bring Professor al-Bardi's translation?"

Cassia thought that an excellent suggestion. But once she was actually seated at a worktable in the small, secluded room below deck, she had second thoughts.

What had given her the idea that she could maneuver Tristan into revealing his true feelings, or that, if she did, she would like what she discovered?

Her cheeks paled as she considered that he might simply be amused to discover her attraction to him. Worse yet, he could put it down to frustration and pity her.

Veda hummed quietly beside her, scanning the papyrus. Cassia cast a glance at her, wishing she could somehow plumb the computer's data banks for information on how to handle her predicament.

But Veda knew only what Cassia herself had taught her, and that meant that in the area of male-female relations she was sadly lacking.

Too fidgety to sit still, Cassia rose and wandered over to the porthole, looking out at the expanse of clear blue sea stretching away to the horizon. Even so far from shore, it was still warm and muggy.

She wished she'd had time to shower and change after completing her journey. There was no opportunity for that now, but at least she could make herself more comfortable.

In her cabin, she hastily dug in her luggage and found a brush. Moments later she had managed to smooth her hair and generally restore some sense of order to her appearance.

Glancing down at herself, she confirmed that her snug white jeans and T-shirt still looked fairly neat without noticing how they emphasized the slender curves of her body.

The small amount of makeup she had put on that morning was long gone, but that didn't seem to matter. Her thick-fringed eyes were unusually bright and dark, while lips she had bitten in her nervousness pouted softly.

Looking in the mirror above the tiny sink, she shook her head disconsolately. If only she were more . . . glamorous. Like Allegra. Her friend would know exactly how to handle this situation.

But then, she was an expert at handling people, hence her successful public relations business, while all Cassia knew were machines and the cold, dry echoes of other people's words.

Feeling sorry for herself wouldn't accomplish anything. Squaring her shoulders, which had the added but unnoticed effect of thrusting her high, firm breasts into even greater prominence, she marched back to the lab.

The murmur of voices drew her up short. Tristan was standing at the worktable conversing with Veda.

"Once we get started on the dives," he said, "maybe we can rig up some way to connect you to the underwater cameras so you can see what's going on down there."

"That would be nice," Veda admitted a bit tentatively. She was clearly still wary of him, but willing to accept a friendly overture. "Of course, Cassia would have to approve."

"Naturally. Where is she, by the way?"

"In her cabin . . . probably fussing with herself."

Tristan's startled laugh did not drown out Cassia's groan as she strode into the lab. Angrily, she snapped, "That's quite enough. You've got a job to do."

"Don't be mad at her," Tristan cajoled. "She was just answering my question." Archly, he added, "Isn't that what she's programmed to do?"

It was, but that hardly improved matters. Veda was perfectly capable of responding to inquiries with only the barest amount of information when she chose to do so.

Her cooperativeness seemed to be dependent on how she felt about the person asking the questions. Clearly, she had decided that Tristan wasn't so bad after all, and that it wouldn't hurt for her to extend herself a bit for him.

"I think I'd better try to add some sense of discretion to that program," Cassia muttered. "Otherwise, she'll be shooting off about all sorts of things."

Veda blinked irately but did not comment. Figuratively turning her back on them, she resumed scanning the papyrus.

After a moment, Tristan said, "I brought along al-Bardi's translation and comments. I hope they'll be of some help."

Cassia had taken the papers he offered and was glancing through them. After a moment she looked up, puzzled. "The professor did a very thorough job. Even without his presence, you shouldn't have any problem finding the location indicated here."

He raised an eyebrow challengingly. "So?"

"So . . . why did you ask me to join the expedition?"

Good question, Tristan thought wryly. He'd thought he knew the answer, but lately he'd begun to wonder. Finding her with Hank had made him abruptly aware of his feelings.

She'd only been on board a few hours and already the neat rationale he'd created, that he only wanted them to work together, was beginning to crumble.

"Just because al-Bardi did such a good job," he hedged, "doesn't mean another linguist shouldn't take a look at the same material. Anyone can miss something, and if he did, you may spot it."

Running a hand through his hair, he added, "Anyway, suppose we start bringing up artifacts with inscriptions on them? They might reveal whether or not we'd really found Atlantis and if we should go on looking."

Cassia listened to him gravely. His explanation made sense, but only up to a point. *Questor*'s sophisticated communications equipment could easily have relayed photographs of any inscribed artifacts to the museum or university of his choice.

He could have had his pick of scholars to decipher them. For that matter, just about any linguist she could think of would have jumped at the chance to accompany the expedition. Yet he had asked her.

Busy telling herself not to read too much into that, Cassia missed his unguarded expression. Tristan was taking advantage of her preoccupation to study her bemusedly.

With her hair lying in soft tendrils around her lightly freckled face, she looked like a vulnerable child. But there was nothing childlike about the curves revealed by the white jeans and T-shirt. Or about the sensuality of her soft, full mouth that seemed to beckon to him.

Hardly aware that he did so, he leaned forward slightly, breathing in the delicate scent of her. She smelled of lemons and honeysuckle and pure, wholesome woman.

He had a quick mental image of a sun-washed field of wild flowers waving in the breeze, and of himself lying there beside her, the two of them lost in a private world of their own creation.

Almost desperately, he tried to muster his usual cynicism. In thirty-four years he had seen too much of the darker side of life to still nurture any illusions. Or so he had thought.

Cassia made him wonder if his carefully limited expectations might be overdue for expansion. Was it really possible for a man and a woman to do more than simply satisfy each other's physical needs? Could there really be the kind of romantic love he had always scoffed at, but which he now found himself almost yearning for?

His mouth tightened as a flare of resentment darted through him. He didn't want to desire anything whose fulfillment was so intrinsically dependent on the actions of another person.

His life had taught him to be self-sufficient and to

keep himself emotionally unencumbered. To do otherwise was to invite the terrible pain he remembered all too well from his childhood.

Gazing down at her, seeing the softness of her eyes and mouth, the slight flush of her cheeks, and the rapid rise and fall of her breasts, he realized that she must be aware—at least on some level—of how she tempted him. But she showed no sign of caring that he might be hurt.

Like a very young girl determined to test her powers, she was placing him in danger without a qualm. Grimly, he decided that under such circumstances there was no reason not to satisfy her curiosity about herself.

He would take what she offered and no doubt discover that the dream she seemed to represent was as shallow as everything else he had found in his relationships with women. Recognizing that, he would be immune, safe from any further threat.

So ran his thinking as his burnished hands reached out to grasp Cassia's shoulders and draw her to him. Her eyes widened slightly in surprise, but she made no effort to pull back.

When he had kissed her the evening they met, Tristan had used all his expertise to set her trembling in his arms. Now he did not bother with any such artfulness.

His intent was to satisfy himself, without thought of her. If she was frightened in the process, so much the better. Perhaps then she would keep her distance and let him get on with his life.

An unholy light flared in his sea-green eyes as his

proud head bent. With none of the coaxing gentleness he had used before, he claimed her mouth.

Cassia's gasp was stifled by the hard pressure of his lips. Her own were opened ruthlessly to admit the probing shaft of his tongue.

As he deepened that intimate caress, his hands slid down the long length of her back to close round her firm buttocks and pull her ruthlessly against him.

It was too much, too fast. Cassia instinctively rebelled. Her fists pushed against the unyielding wall of his chest as she tried to squirm away.

Her efforts had no effect except to further heighten his arousal. He broke off the kiss long enough to mutter cynically, "That's it, honey. Make it good for me."

Outrage tore through her, banishing even the fear sparked by the realization of how helpless she was against his strength. How dare he treat her like this, as though she were some woman he'd bought to please him!

Instinctively, she bent her leg and brought her knee up firmly against him. Had Tristan's reflexes been anything less than superb, he would have been greatly discomfited, at the very least. But as it was, he eluded her blow and laughed callously.

"You can't seem to make up your mind how to play this. Maybe I'd better just do it for you."

Though he spoke quietly, those words were enough to freeze Cassia. Whether it was intentional or not, she heard the implied threat and for an instant was paralyzed.

Then the outrage she had felt a moment before

flooded back, amplified a hundred times. A sound rippled deep in her throat, the growl of a feline roused to deadly anger.

"You bastard," she grated harshly. "Let me go!"

He went very still. A taut, white line appeared around his mouth, and a feral glitter darkened his eyes.

Too late, she remembered what Allegra had told her about him and realized the implications of what she had said.

"Tristan . . . I-I didn't mean . . ."

He showed no sign of having heard her. That, more than anything, transformed her angry fear into outright terror.

His utter self-containment and absolute concentration on what he was about to do left no room for any awareness of her as a person.

At that moment, she was simply the cause of his pain, and the instrument for easing it.

One big hand continued to hold her buttocks against him while the other tangled in her hair, dragging her head back and forcing her to meet his contemptuous stare.

He could see the frantic pulse beating in the hollow at the base of her throat, feel the surge of shock and fear darting through her.

So slowly that she had ample time to consider what he was about to do, he lowered his head and pressed his mouth to that tremulous flutter. Lingering there, he tasted the sweetness of her skin and the rhythmic pulsing of her life's blood.

A wave of heat washed over Cassia, making her tremble. She had girded herself for violence, only to encounter a ruthless sexual expertise that left her dazed.

She was only dimly aware of being picked up and carried from the lab the short distance to her cabin. Tristan's warm, seeking mouth continued to wander over her as he stepped adroitly around the scattered luggage and laid her on the narrow bunk.

Before she could think to resist, he lowered himself on top of her, using his far greater weight and strength to press her into the mattress. His hands cupped her face, the thumbs pressing with unexpected gentleness at her lips.

"Open your mouth for me, Cassia," he groaned thickly.

Overcome by the incredible sensations spiraling through her, she did as he said. This time his kiss was hauntingly tender, sipping at her slightly swollen mouth until she thought she would go mad with wanting more.

Tristan raised his head for a moment, staring down at her with hard, glittering scrutiny. As he took in the tumbled disarray of her hair, her shining eyes, and the ripe fullness of her lips, he laughed knowingly.

Something in that sound distressed Cassia. She moaned softly and tried to twist away, only to be stopped by his hands sliding beneath her T-shirt to deftly caress her breasts.

The thin lace of her bra offered scant protection,

as Tristan clearly understood. He rubbed the slightly abrasive fabric sensuously against her nipples until they were taut and aching.

"Please . . ." Cassia gasped, hardly aware of what she was saying. "D-don't . . ."

Tristan ignored her. His iron-hard thighs kept her in place as he slid the T-shirt over her head and tossed it to the floor.

The front catch of her bra delayed him only momentarily. Then it too was gone and she lay fully exposed to his gaze.

"My God . . ." he moaned raggedly, "you're so lovely. . . ." The words were torn from him. He did not want to be so moved by her delicate beauty, but he was powerless to control his response to her.

Driven by needs he could not control, he buried his head between her breasts. The scent and warmth of her engulfed him even as her slender arms rose, hesitated a moment, then closed around him.

So many contradictory emotions had assailed Cassia in the last few minutes—anger, passion, fear, joy—that one more seemed in no way surprising. A surge of almost maternal gentleness rushed through her as she cradled him to her.

"Tristan . . . let's not be cruel to each other . . . that's so senseless. . . ."

His answer was to draw her even closer, his hands kneading and caressing her breasts until she cried out softly. His warm, wet tongue circled each aching nipple, licking the taut peaks before drawing first one and then the other into his mouth to be gently suckled.

His touch seemed to reach directly into the hot, moist core of her, rousing it to full, throbbing life. Her hips arched instinctively against him, seeking the straining hardness of his manhood through the layers of fabric still separating them.

Her silver-blond head tossed widely across the pillows. She was in pain, yet she had never known such pleasure. She wanted . . . something she could barely sense, yet which she must have or she would surely die.

The man above her was the key to it all. Only he could give her what she so desperately needed.

Without releasing her nipple, Tristan moved slightly to give his hand access to the soft cleft at the apex of her thighs. His fingers moved skillfully, drawing a sharp cry of astonished delight from her.

In a detached, clinical sense, Cassia understood that a woman could be aroused to a peak of sexual need that, ideally, culminated in the release of fulfillment. But knowing that had in no way prepared her for the actual experience.

She felt as though her body and soul were gathering themselves into a single force, growing stronger and more vital with each wave of pleasure, until they must surely explode.

Fear of the approaching cataclysm made her try to draw back, but Tristan would not allow it. He broke off his caresses only long enough to yank open the snap of her jeans, push the zipper down, and slip his hand in past the barrier of her lacy underpants.

He did not question his motives as his fingers deftly parted the moist curls sheltering her womanhood and resumed their devastating rhythm. All thought of hurting or punishing her had vanished.

He wanted only to give her the most transcendent pleasure a woman could experience, without demanding anything from her in return.

His lips took hers hungrily, his tongue thrusting into her mouth at the same instant that his thumb began to tease the small, tight opening to her.

Cassia no longer doubted that she was about to die, but she didn't seem to mind. Instead she was driven to give him some measure of the same incandescent delight he was showering so generously on her.

Her hands shook as she undid the buttons of his khaki shirt. That simple task almost defeated her, but at last it was done and she was free to explore the taut, sinewy smoothness of his chest. As her fingers pressed lightly against his flat male nipples, Tristan bit back a groan.

"Witch . . . you're driving me insane!"

Cassia heard him through the dazzling light of her own pleasure, and smiled languorously. She wanted to push him past the barriers of self-control to the same realm she was inexorably entering, but with only instinct to guide her, she was not sure how to proceed.

At any rate, there was no chance, for Tristan increased the pace and intensity of his caresses. His calloused fingers closed around the ultrasensitive bud of her desire, pressing and kneading even as his knee pushed between her soft legs, opening her further for him.

He shifted slightly, just enough to slide her jeans and panties down farther and give his other hand access to the throbbing passage of her womanhood.

Long, hard fingers slid carefully into her, pausing to make sure he caused her no pain, going only so far as she could comfortably accommodate him and no farther.

The effect was devastating. She was more vividly aware than ever of the aching emptiness within her. Arching helplessly against his hand, she cried out hoarsely.

"Tristan . . . help me . . . please. . . ."

"I will, beautiful witch," he rasped. "Trust me."

Despite the spiraling waves of ecstasy gripping her, Cassia still understood what he was saying. To achieve what she so frantically needed, she had to surrender herself completely to his care. Only then would the terrible pressure within her be relieved.

Pride and the intrinsic fear of giving herself so utterly to someone else held her back. She was trapped between two equally unacceptable alternatives, and had no way to save herself.

That was left to Tristan. He realized her quandary and chose not to leave her in it. With a muffled curse, he pushed her jeans and panties the rest of the way down her legs, tearing them off along with her sandals.

Sliding lower in the bunk, he gripped her buttocks in his hands and compelled her to accept a caress that wrung a gasp of shock from her, followed quickly by a cry of unendurable ecstasy.

The world and everything in it, save for the man

who held her, ceased to exist for Cassia. There was only Tristan and the incredible rapture he was unleashing within her.

Again and again he drove her relentlessly to the brink of release before finally hurling her over it into a realm where all thought ceased and only radiant sensation existed.

She came back to the real world slowly and reluctantly, with a dazed sense of having traveled an immense distance. Tristan lay above her, smiling down into her flushed face, his gaze gentle.

But Cassia didn't see that. She saw only that he appeared amused, and that she was horribly, devastatingly vulnerable to him.

How could she have behaved so wantonly? How could she have allowed such intimacies with a man who had begun them in anger?

Shame darkened her cheeks and made her lips tremble. Unable to look at him, she turned her head away, unaware that her tears were wetting the pillow.

Tristan let out a sharp exclamation. Since he had entered her only with his fingers, he was reasonably certain he had not caused her any pain. Yet she seemed devastated.

Raggedly, he said, "Cassia . . . don't cry . . . it's all right. . . ."

All right for whom? she wondered dazedly. He had stripped her of her pride and her innocence, exposing her to a world of delights that, in a single instant, had become addictive.

How could she bear to do without such overwhelming pleasure, yet how could she even contemplate subjecting herself again to what seemed like his scornful dominance?

Bitterly, she remembered the contemptuous look on his face when they had argued in the lab. She had called him a bastard, something she deeply regretted. And he had retaliated with all the cunning of his ruthless nature.

The tears flowed more freely as she buried her head in the pillow. Her muffled words barely reached him. "Go away . . . you've done enough. . . ."

Tristan's face tightened. He was deeply wounded by her apparent rejection.

Certainly she had a right to be angry with him for his earlier behavior, but didn't what had passed between them since then make up for it? Did he mean so little to her that she could accept the pleasure he gave, then callously dismiss him from her bed?

Muttering a curse, he rose from the bunk and strode to the door. His hand was on the knob when he glanced back at her, his gaze softening somewhat at the sight of her slender body curled into a dejected heap wracked by sobs.

How he had hurt her, he could not imagine. But she seemed determined to think the worst of him.

With a sigh of deep regret, he left the cabin. The door shut behind him with a click of finality that resounded through the tiny room as vividly as a gunshot tearing through the heart.

Chapter 7

CASSIA DID NOT REMAIN ON THE BUNK LONG. DESPITE the satiation of her body, she could not stay still. With her cheeks streaked by tears and her eyes burning, she padded into the tiny bathroom and turned on the shower full force.

It helped a little. Long moments spent under the rush of cool water restored some sense of self-possession and enabled her to consider what had just happened without shying away in panic.

Was there a special word for a woman who was still technically a virgin but had experienced what must surely be the heights of sensual fulfillment? She bit her lip as a number of possibilities occurred to her—flirt and tease among the kindest.

Yet had she really asked for what had happened,

or had Tristan taken it upon himself to punish her outburst in a particularly vicious way?

Genuinely bewildered and in no condition to puzzle out the truth, she dressed in fresh jeans and a loose cotton shirt, then returned to the lab.

Before very long she would have to join the rest of the crew for dinner, but for the moment her work on the papyrus provided her with a welcome excuse for remaining below deck.

Veda blinked as she took her place at the worktable. "I was getting worried," the computer said. "You and Tristan were behaving so . . . oddly right before you left."

"We were having a little difference of opinion," Cassia said, not caring to elaborate.

But Veda wouldn't let it rest there. She was programmed to seek out knowledge, and this was a subject that puzzled her greatly. "Do humans always hold and kiss each other when they're arguing?"

"No . . . and if you don't mind, I'd rather not talk about it."

"Oh . . . all right." Veda fell silent, only her blinking red light indicating her bewilderment.

Cassia felt a stab of guilt. She had no right to take her problems out on Veda, who, after all, was only doing her job. That was tantamount to getting mad at a child for trying to satisfy its natural curiosity.

"I'm sorry . . . I didn't mean to snap at you."

"There's nothing to apologize for," Veda said gently. "I was intruding on your privacy."

Cassia's breath drew in sharply. A tingling rush of

excitement tore through her, eclipsing for the moment even her concern about Tristan.

So simple a statement, yet so significant. All on her own, Veda had made a critical breakthrough.

She had realized that she and Cassia were not one and the same. They were separate entities who inevitably could not share everything. That sense of being apart did not normally occur in a child until it had reached the age of several years. Yet here it was in Veda, one of the most essential ingredients of intelligence . . . and humanness.

"Veda . . ." Cassia began tentatively, "when did you learn about the need for privacy?"

"I'm not sure . . . exactly. Perhaps when I saw you and Tristan together."

"W-what did that have to do with it?"

"The way you were seemed so intense and so . . . personal. It wasn't right for anyone else to be involved."

Cassia blushed at that. If Veda—with no experience in such matters and no basis for comparison—had sensed the explosive passion between them, it must have been truly extraordinary.

Unable to confront the truth of that just yet, she said, "Let's get back to the papyrus, all right?"

Veda concurred, and for the next several hours they worked together to confirm Professor al-Bardi's translation, as well as the coordinates he had plotted as a result of the details given by the Pharaoh's envoy.

That last part was the most difficult. Prevailing winds and currents had to be taken into account, as did the state of shipbuilding and navigational skills at the time of the ancient journey.

Cassia had never been so grateful for Veda's massive data banks as she was then. The conclusion that had taken the professor months of work to reach was hers in a matter of hours. His coordinates, in her opinion, were accurate.

Not that this necessarily meant *Questor*'s search would be successful. It wasn't beyond the realm of possibility that the papyrus was a fake. A very ancient one, certainly, but still a fake.

She couldn't imagine why anyone forty-five hundred years ago would have gone to the trouble of devising such a thing, but then people had been dreaming up stories and writing them down for ages. Who was to say this wasn't simply a very early example of the human need to record its imaginings?

Should that turn out to be the case, the expedition was destined for failure. Yet if the document was factual, the discovery they made would shake the scientific and scholarly worlds to their very foundations.

Trust Tristan to take on something so potentially explosive. She wondered if he ever did anything ordinary, and decided that was highly unlikely. But then, why should he, when he had remarkable resources at his command.

Unwilling though she was to do so, Cassia knew that sooner or later she would have to confront what had happened between them in her cabin. The encounter baffled her.

Tristan had been lividly angry at the beginning,

she was certain of that. Try though she might, she couldn't find it in herself to blame him. Honesty forced her to admit that she had behaved with deliberate, if rather inept, provocativeness.

But his rage hadn't lasted long. It had given way swiftly to . . . what? Her fear that he had simply taunted her with his control of her body did not stand up too well under examination.

It was hardly a punishment to be made vividly, gloriously aware of her capacity for pleasure. Especially not by a man who—she had to admit—had dealt with her gently and patiently, demanding nothing for himself and giving everything.

Cassia sighed deeply, wishing she knew which was real—the cruel, vengeful Tristan, or the loving, passionate one. So much hinged on that. Yet she could think of no way to solve the puzzle except . . .

A slight flush stained her cheeks as she considered what seemed to be her only alternative. Surely she couldn't . . .?

Her chin lifted, and a determined light shone in her blue-gray eyes. A glance at the clock on the lab wall showed her that it was time to join the others for dinner. Schooling her features into what she hoped was a serene expression, she headed for the mess.

The long, narrow room contained a gleaming refectory table large enough to seat the entire crew. The table was sensibly bolted to the floor and had a rim all around it to contain wayward dishes. Comfortable chairs and other, smaller tables for playing cards, chess, and so on were similarly outfitted.

Shelves along one wall held an eclectic collection of books and records.

Most of the crew was already there, laughing and talking among themselves. Cassia hesitated a moment, feeling out of place, until Jason Lombard saw her and called a welcome.

"Come on in, doctor. We were just wondering how you're doing with the papyrus." He rose from his place at the table and held out a chair for her as the other men nodded respectfully and Hank grinned with his usual exuberance.

Sending Jason an appreciative smile, Cassia took her seat. She was grateful for the veneer of professional camaraderie that readily enfolded her. "I've completed the analysis, and Professor al-Bardi's translation certainly seems to be accurate, as does his deduction of the coordinates where we'll be searching."

"So you think we're on the right track?" Hank asked eagerly.

"It appears that way," she agreed cautiously. "Of course, there are still many imponderables, but right now it looks promising." She had already decided that no good could come from mentioning her concern that the papyrus might be a work of fiction.

That would serve no purpose but to dampen their enthusiasm just when they were going to need it most. A quick glance in Jason's direction showed her that the same thought had occurred to him, but he, too, chose not to speak of it.

Talk shifted to the complexities of winds and tides, and the all-important weather reports that predicted calm seas and skies for at least the next week. They were deep into a discussion of diving equipment when Cassia suddenly felt a shiver run up her spine.

Without turning around, she knew that Tristan had arrived. Jason confirmed that a moment later.

"So you finally decided to take a break," the archaeologist teased. "We were about to start without you."

The quiet voice that responded set her nerves on edge. "You should have. I got bogged down on some navigational checks."

"Everything okay?" one of the divers asked.

Tristan nodded as he took a seat across from Cassia and flicked an inscrutable glance in her direction. "We're on course and on schedule." He smiled slightly. "You guys better not get too comfortable. We'll be at the diving site by tomorrow."

"Can't come soon enough for me," Hank declared, making no secret of his eagerness to get on with the adventure.

An older, more experienced diver laughed. "We'll see how you feel a week from now. I've been on digs like this when it took a hundred dives or more to turn up the first artifact. You'll be bone tired and wet most of the time, and after a while you'll start seeing things down there."

Despite himself, Hank's eyes widened slightly. "Like what?"

"Hard to say, exactly . . . shapes of things that aren't real . . . skeletons . . . that sort of thing."

The young man gulped, prompting amused laughter. Tristan let it run its course before he said matter-of-factly, "We certainly won't be finding any bodies, unless we stumble on a recent wreck. The best I'm hoping for is stonework, and perhaps some shards of pottery."

Hank looked decidedly relieved. He grinned abashedly and, when dinner arrived a moment later, dug in along with all the rest.

The food, Cassia quickly discovered, was excellent. Avocado soup was followed by succulent chicken cooked with coconut and curry and accompanied by sautéed plantains.

Ordinarily, she would have relished the exotic dishes. But under the circumstances, she found it impossible to swallow more than a few bites of each.

Though she was careful not to look at Tristan, she was vividly aware of his presence. The deep timber of his voice as he spoke with the men resonated through her.

From the corner of her eye, she watched his smooth movements as though mesmerized by them. Once he laughed and the sound made her jerk.

"Are you all right, Cassia?" Jason asked concernedly.

"Of course."

"You don't seem to be enjoying dinner. Too spicy for you?"

Acutely aware that everyone's attention was focused on her, she murmured, "No, it's delicious. I'm just . . ."

As she fumbled for some plausible explanation,

Jason smiled sympathetically. "Not got your sea legs yet? That's natural. Maybe some fresh air would help."

Seizing the excuse, Cassia stood up. "I think you're right." She glanced around the table without meeting Tristan's eye. "If you'll all excuse me . . ."

To their murmured words of sympathy, she departed, hastily making her way on deck, where she sought a secluded spot far in the prow of the ship. From there she could watch the last remnants of what had been a glorious sunset.

Wisps of cerise and gold lingered at the western horizon along the edge of a sky turning from navy blue to black. A pale half-moon haunted the heavens, little competition for the riot of stars coming into view.

No sound disturbed her thoughts save for the low, rhythmic throbbing of *Questor*'s powerful engines, the lapping of water against the prow, and the satiny whisper of a southeast wind fresh and clean with the scents of salt and sun. Lingering beneath them, she fancied she could still smell the perfumes of land, blooming plants and fecund earth.

Tomorrow, she promised herself, and for as long as she was on board *Questor*, she would make sure not to miss the spectacle of day's end. For too long she had ignored the world's beauty. In this time and place, she would begin at last to savor it.

As lovely as the gathering night was, it cried out to be shared. Cassia stirred restlessly, trying to still the hollow sense of loneliness within her.

She had always been so self-sufficient, and her new and growing state of dependency left her baffled. Some glimmer of what Tristan might have felt when they stood together in the lab reached her as she considered how fine a line there was between resentment and attraction, fear and desire, hate and love.

Alone on the deck, Cassia strove to quiet the clamoring of her mind and let the peace of her surroundings seep into her. She closed her eyes and breathed slowly and deeply.

Long moments passed, how many she could not have said, before she emerged from the cocoon of quietude to the awareness that she was no longer alone.

Just as she had in the galley, she knew that Tristan was near. Something . . . electrical flowed between them, needing neither sight nor sound to confirm its presence.

Her eyes opened, the pupils dilated in the darkness. She stood perfectly still, drinking in the sight of him without restraint.

The khaki pants and shirt he wore were comfortably loose but could in no way disguise the lean hardness of his body. His bare feet had been slid into topsiders that allowed him to move agilely and silently along the deck.

Night's shadows obscured his features, but she could feel the intensity of his gaze and knew that any attempt on her part to elude him would meet with failure.

He had come seeking . . . what? Cassia barely breathed, waiting for him to disclose the direction of his thoughts.

Tristan had been watching her from a distance for some time before he stepped forward to reveal himself. Unbeknown to her, he had shared her pleasure in the sunset even though, to his eyes at least, it could not rival the loveliness of silver-blond hair, apricot-tinged skin, and a strong, slender body that stood with unconscious dignity.

It had not escaped his attention that his usual self-confidence was missing. He was very hesitant about approaching her, uncertain of his reception and all too aware that if she rounded on him angrily, he would be badly hurt.

Yet for all that he could not regret what had happened in her cabin. She had never appeared more beautiful to him than at that moment when she first experienced the full, unbridled pleasure of a woman.

Her surprise—more correctly, her shock—had not escaped him. Every suspicion he had had about her innocence was vividly reaffirmed, leaving him at even more of a loss as to how to deal with her.

But cope he must, for he truly had no choice. In the hours since that encounter, he had reluctantly faced the fact that all his carefully constructed defenses were, if not completely gone, at least seriously eroded.

Whatever the risk, he had to at least try to come to terms with her. An iota of tension eased from him as he considered the irony of that.

He who had always mocked the rituals of courtship, preferring instead the simplicity of sex free of commitment, was about to entangle himself up to his very neck with an exasperating creature of uncertain temperament and unknown intentions.

So much for his vaunted intelligence! Smothering a sigh, Tristan moved toward her as cautiously as he would approach a wild doe poised for flight.

In the quiet of the night, amid the solitude of the sea, the dance began . . . its steps the movements of two bodies and its music the carefully contained hopes of two minds and hearts.

"Cassia . . . I don't mean to disturb you, but . . . we need to talk."

"Yes . . . it's all right. . . . I know we do. . . ."

"About . . . before . . . I'm sorry . . . I didn't mean for any of that to happen."

Not any? Did that mean his gift of pleasure had been unintentional? How she hoped not!

"You were . . . angry with me. Rightfully. Please forgive me for what I said."

Did that mean she knew? How? Allegra, of course. Relief at not having to tell her himself slid through Tristan. He managed a weak smile. "I should be used to being called a bastard by now, but it's still like waving a red flag in front of me."

"I spoke before I could consider how it would hurt you. With another man, I might have remembered, but with you . . ."

"What makes me different?" he asked, genuinely puzzled.

Her laughter was soft, yet heartfelt. "Everything! I've never met anyone remotely like you."

His mouth, drawn so tightly a short time before, turned up at the corners. "Has it occurred to you that I'm in the same boat?"

She stared at him for a long moment, wanting to believe, yet not quite daring to. At last, she whispered, "Are you . . .?"

He moved closer to her, not yet touching, but near enough for her to feel the warmth of his skin through the thin layers of khaki and cotton separating them.

His voice was so low as to be a caress. "Oh, yes, I rather think so. We're two of a kind, Cassia. Out of step with the rest of the world and compelled to make our own way. It's a lonely business, isn't it?"

She blinked, feeling the heat of unshed tears beneath her lids. Not trusting her voice, she could only nod.

He studied her for a long moment with an intensity that did not allow her to look away. Ruefully, he wished he could analyze her as he did so much else. But she remained a mystery to him, a beautiful, elusive dream as haunting as the pale moon riding far above them.

She wanted him, he was certain of that now. But the ruthless honesty that characterized his life forced him to admit that her desire might be sparked by nothing more than natural curiosity.

She had lived all her life in an environment that gave the mind free rein while hemming in the body and spirit. Now, at last, intelligence was being matched by instinct.

Once he had called her a princess. That still seemed apt. But the tower that had held her was crumbling.

Not for a moment was he so arrogant as to think that was his doing. Cassia was remaking herself, perhaps spurred on by him, but still in control of what she was to become.

He might be no more to her than the means to an end. If that were the case, the pain he had known in the past was destined to be utterly eclipsed by what lay ahead.

Yet even realizing the risk, he could not pull back. The memory of her sweet, abandoned beauty as they lay together in the cabin overwhelmed him.

His big, capable hands shook slightly as he reached for her.

Chapter 8

THE SENSATION OF BEING ONCE AGAIN IN TRISTAN'S arms was unlike anything Cassia had ever experienced. There was still all the excitement of newness, but beneath it, tremulous yet unmistakable, was a sense of homecoming so sweet as to bring tears to her eyes.

She pressed her face into his chest, loving the solid warmth beneath her cheek and the steady beat of his heart, growing more urgent with each passing moment.

The unique scent of him—a combination of the lightly spiced after-shave he wore, the salty tang of the sea, and the intrinsic musk of virility—made the muscles of her abdomen clench.

Through her thin T-shirt, she could feel the slight abrasiveness of his calloused hands moving gently along her back. The entire length of his body was taut with need, yet he held himself still, giving her time to come to terms with what was happening.

Secure in his embrace, she marveled at how his touch alone instantly brought her desire for him to almost unbearable limits yet, paradoxically, removed all sense of urgency. Safe in the sheltering darkness of the starry night, they seemed to have all the time in the world.

She tilted her head back, gazing up at him with eyes glazed by gathering passion—and concern. "Tristan . . . this is real, isn't it?"

His arms tightened around her. "What else could it be?"

"A dream that can't be realized . . . a chimera."

"What a sad thought. Everything around us, everything we know and experience, was once no more than a dream."

Her smile was wistful.

"Suddenly you're a philosopher."

"No," he corrected quietly, "a realist. There are no guarantees, only possibilities."

Cassia shivered. He was right. She had lived all her life sheltered from risks. The only options presented to her had been well within her grasp. Now, for the first time, she wanted something that might prove unattainable.

Looking up at him, she wondered what he thought about that. His eyes were hooded, his expression carefully contained. But as she watched, a ragged pulse leaped to life in his jaw, betraying his own vulnerability.

Rising slightly on her toes, she touched her lips gently to the place where his life's blood raced so desperately. A tremor ran through him. His fingers splayed out along her back, pressing her even closer.

Yielding to instincts she had not known she possessed, she pursued her advantage. Her lips drifted along the hollowed plane of his cheek, tracing the contours of his square chin, lingering in the slight cleft that was almost, but not quite, a dimple, before at last finding their way without haste to the corner of his mouth.

Tristan endured it as long as he could. He wanted to give her every opportunity to set the pace for them both, and to begin to learn the full extent of her womanly powers.

But he was, after all, only a man, and the sweet torture she inflicted on him quickly became too much to bear. A low growl broke from him as his arms closed like iron bands around her.

His hand grasped the nape of her neck beneath the feathery tendrils of her hair. Gently but with implacable demand he bent her head back.

For a moment out of time they stood like that, silently asking questions words could not answer. In her flushed face, parted lips, and innocently candid gaze, Tristan saw all that he wanted to believe in and more he could not yet understand.

Something far beyond mere sexual desire was stirring within him. More powerful even than the throbbing demand of his loins was the rush of possessiveness that swept over him as he studied her.

Never had he wanted a woman so desperately. No

other consideration could override his determination to make her his, not simply for a night or a week or a month, but to stamp her forever as his own.

Cassia sensed his fierce resolution and knew that she should be frightened by it, but instead she could feel only a heady sense of exhilaration. He wanted her, as she did him. For the moment, that was enough.

A low, utterly feminine laugh rippled from her. Deliberately, she moved in his arms to shatter the last of his restraint.

"I was right to name you a witch," he muttered. "You spin magic . . . like moonbeams . . . a fog in my mind. . . ."

"It's not my spell," she breathed. "We're both caught. . . ."

His mouth closed over hers, capturing the words that were almost a plea. Her lips parted willingly, her tongue stroking over the rough surface of his.

Together they tasted, savored, teased, promised, until the very deck seemed to quake beneath their feet and Tristan at last raised his head shakily.

"This isn't the place . . ." He broke off, waiting.

Cassia knew what he was doing, giving her a last chance to back away. If she did not, what happened would be as much her responsibility as his.

She accepted that willingly, knowing that anything else would be intolerable. "My cabin . . ."

Tristan did not need to hear more. He bent slightly, placing one arm behind her knees and the other around her back.

She was just about to tell him that she was not

some will-o'-the-wisp to be easily toted around, when her feet left the deck and she found herself securely nestled high against his chest.

A bit breathlessly, she murmured, "You must have been a pirate in another life."

Grinning ingenuously, Tristan strode toward the hatch. "I'm addicted to Errol Flynn movies."

"Me too! I've seen *Captain Blood* a dozen times."

"How did you manage that in the ivory tower?"

A bit breathlessly, she explained, "Veda monitors all the regular television broadcasts. I started watching with her because I thought it would be educational."

"And was it?" he inquired, stooping slightly to open the door of her cabin. He stepped inside and kicked it closed, then strode over to her bed.

There he hesitated, remembering what had happened in this same place only a few hours before and wanting this time to be different so that it might also be better.

"Very," Cassia murmured as he sat down, cradling her in his lap. Startled, she laughed softly. "Have I tired you already?"

A potently male light of challenge flickered in his eyes. "No, but you'll realize that soon enough." More gently, he added, "You're so beautiful, Cassia, both inside and out. I never want to do anything to hurt you."

She swallowed tightly. "You won't, I'm sure."

Silently, Tristan wished she had added that she would try not to harm him. It was on the tip of his tongue to ask her, but he could not. Somehow it wasn't quite manly to confess that he feared what would happen to his heart once it was given fully into her small hands.

As the warmth of her body seeped into his, he reminded himself that she had far more to fear than he, at least this first time. He was certain she had never been with a man before. That knowledge made him feel oddly humble, and determined to make the experience all that it should be for her.

Rather wryly, he considered his own initiation to lovemaking. Or, more correctly, to sex.

He'd been fifteen at the time, kicked out of his most recent foster home and about to run away for the last time from the state orphanage. There had been no question of love between him and the older, experienced girl who had claimed his virginity on a mat in a corner of a supply room.

In some ways, the encounter had been quite satisfying. He'd come away feeling relieved, proud, and eager for more. But in the back of his mind there had been a sense of something important missing.

Back then he hadn't even been able to give a name to whatever it was he wished for, but now he knew. Sex without a genuine sense of caring was no more than the rutting of two healthy young animals. The human spirit was capable of far more.

An unaccustomedly gentle smile curved his mouth. He could feel her growing more tense against him. She was nervous, but also eager. He would build on the second while erasing the first.

Without questioning his motives, he made the

decision to curb his own impatience and go slowly no matter what the cost to him.

Was she supposed to be doing something? Cassia wondered as moments passed and Tristan made no effort to begin their lovemaking.

She was acutely conscious of his hardened manhood pressing against her rounded bottom. Clearly he wanted her, yet he seemed in no hurry to proceed.

If he expected her to know what to do, he was in for a disappointment. Beyond the biological rudiments and what she had gleaned in their earlier encounter, she was woefully ignorant.

She nibbled nervously at her lower lip, worrying that he might find her inept and boring.

"Tristan . . ."

Distracted by the slight wiggle of her bottom against him, he answered absently. "Hmmm . . . ?"

"I just thought you should know I haven't . . . done much of this sort of thing."

"Really?" he drawled. "But you have done some?"

The trace of humor in his tone stiffened Cassia's spine. Defiantly, she said, "Of course. Surely you didn't think I was a complete innocent?"

Tristan frowned. He most certainly *had* thought so, and he still did. Nothing would convince him that her encounters with him did not constitute the sum total of her experience with men.

Her attempt at dissembling could not be allowed to go by uncorrected. There was no place for pretense between them.

In a single motion, he stood and set her on her feet before him. As she looked up, startled, he nodded decisively. "Good. Since you're not a complete ingenue, I don't have to treat you as one. We both know why we're here. Let's get on with it."

Cassia stared at him warily. She didn't know what game he was suddenly playing, but she was sure she didn't like it. Where was the gentle, romantic lover of a moment before?

Defensively, she said, "There's no reason to be crude about it."

He spread his hands innocently. "Who's being crude? We're both adults, answerable to no one but ourselves. Let's enjoy what we've got." As he spoke, he matter-of-factly kicked off his topsiders and followed them swiftly with his shirt.

Cassia watched wide-eyed as he unsnapped the waistband of his slacks. Only when he began to slip the zipper down did she recover her wits. "What are you doing?"

"Getting undressed, of course. I want to make love naked this time. Later we can try all the . . . variations."

"Wait! I don't want to! Not . . . like this."

He paused in the midst of slipping out of his slacks. "No? I'm pretty broad-minded. What did you have in mind?"

"Nothing! That is . . ." She broke off, her face flaming. The situation was getting completely out of hand. From the looks of it, he fully expected her to just strip off her clothes as he was doing and tumble into bed with him.

For all the aching need he sparked in her, she couldn't do that. Intrinsic shyness and uncertainty about her own abilities held her back.

"Tristan . . . I . . ."

He took a step toward her, his hands rubbing warmly up and down her slender arms. "Yesss . . . ?"

Helplessly, she gazed up at him. "Why are you being like this?"

His face clouded. Guilt was an unfamiliar emotion, but one he had no trouble recognizing. "I'm sorry," he muttered thickly. "You made me angry with that claim of being experienced."

"Would it be so wrong if I were?"

"No, of course not. But I don't want you to put up barriers between us. Pretending to be something you're not is a way of doing that."

Cassia's eyes fell. Hesitantly, she said, "It's hard to be completely honest."

His hands tightened on her, not hurting, but letting her feel the impact her words had on him. "I know," he murmured huskily. "You scare me, too."

She must have heard him wrong. He couldn't have said . . . Doubtfully, she asked, "I do?"

He grinned wryly. "Right down to my boots, if I were wearing boots. Honey, you don't realize what a situation like this does to a man like me. I'm used to relationships that are much simpler."

The mention, however oblique, of the other women he had been involved with raised her hackles. "I would think," she said frostily, "that you wouldn't appreciate anything simple."

His rueful laughter was unfeigned. "That's what I mean. You already know so much about me. No other woman has gotten that far."

Mollified, she smiled. "I don't know anywhere near enough." Her voice dropped to a husky caress. "But how I want to . . ."

As though of their own volition, her arms wound around the corded column of his throat. Pressing closer, she let her breasts rub against the hard, bare skin of his chest.

Tristan groaned deep in his throat. His hands slid down to grasp her hips, pulling her nearer. "You will," he promised thickly.

Slowly, holding his great need in tight restraint, he kissed a line of fire down her throat to the delicate curve of her shoulders. There he was stopped by the neckline of her shirt.

"This is in my way," he murmured, tugging it out of her waistband. Docilely as a child, she raised her arms and let him remove the offending garment.

His hands cupped her breasts, the thumbs rubbing slowly over her aroused nipples. So slowly, so repeatedly, that at last she could bear no more.

"Tristan . . . don't tease me this time. I can't stand it."

"Neither of us could," he acknowledged tightly. With a swift movement, her bra was gone, leaving her naked to the waist. Some contrary reflex made her automatically lift her hands to cover herself.

He let her do so, only to cover her hands with his, gently pressing her fingers against her own flesh, all the while watching her every response.

Cassia had never felt like this, never suspected that the body she had always thought of as strictly utilitarian was in fact an object for sensual pleasure, hers as well as his.

Only hours before she had sensed, for the first time, the full depth of her passion. Now she began to become aware of the more subtle nuances of arousal.

Though he touched only her hands, every inch of her skin tingled with awareness of him. He could not continue like this or she would surely go mad.

Driven by her own desperation, Cassia slipped her hands from beneath his, leaving him cupping her breasts, and inched her fingers beneath the open waistband of his slacks, following the tapering line of hair that disappeared into his Jockey shorts.

Daring greatly, she brushed against the rough curls of silk that grew in a thick thatch. Her touch was feather light, but enough to make his hardened manhood swell even further.

Fascinated by the transformation he was undergoing, she was driven to explore farther, only to be stopped by Tristan's swift grasping of her wrist.

"That's enough," he rasped. At her plainly disappointed expression, he laughed gently and added, "For the moment. I don't want to rush this."

Neither did she, yet the mystery unfolding before her was irresistible. She had to know it all, and soon.

A sigh of relief broke from her as he undid her jeans and slipped them from her. Left in nothing but the lacy scrap of her panties, she knew a moment's shyness.

That was silly, considering what had happened earlier. But she couldn't quite fight down her modesty as his eyes wandered over her.

Tristan was a man caught in the throes of a bittersweet struggle. As his gaze swept from her tousled hair down her flushed face with its lovely glowing eyes and ripely soft mouth, he felt all his good intentions dissolving.

The proud tilt of her head and slender grace of her throat enchanted him. Her shoulders were perfectly curved, her arms long and delicate. The ripe silkiness of her breasts with their full, rose-hued nipples sent a spark of pure flame radiating through his loins.

Breathing shakily, he studied the inward arch of her waist, so deep as to make the flare of her slim hips all the more compelling. Above the thin elastic of her last covering, he could see the flat plane of her abdomen dimpled by her navel.

Her legs were long, and as beautifully made as all the rest of her. Slender feet and ankles gave way to shapely calves and lithe thighs shadowed by a triangle of silvery curls.

Dazedly, he remembered how it had felt to kiss and caress her, raising her to a fever pitch of desire. Never had he known so responsive a woman. For better or worse, he had to have her completely.

Raising his eyes to her face again, he saw the tremulous embarrassment there and smiled gently. "There's no reason to be self-conscious, sweetheart. You're an exquisitely beautiful woman."

Holding her eyes with his own, he matter-of-factly

stripped off the rest of his clothes and stood before her proudly naked. His well-shaped feet were planted slightly apart, his hands resting lightly on his hips, his manhood full and ready.

Cassia found it suddenly difficult to breathe. She stared at him in frank fascination. Never had she imagined a man could be so compelling. She longed to go to him, yet a remnant of fear held her back.

Tristan watched the play of emotion across her face and was pleased by it. He was certain now that she truly wanted him, but understood her fear of the strangeness he represented.

Justly confident of his skill as a lover, and of her receptiveness, he knew the time had come to show her that her fears were needless.

Holding out a hand, he commanded softly, "Come here, Cassia."

She hesitated, on the verge of stepping into new, uncharted territory. Behind her was the security of innocence; ahead lay mystery and danger.

For just an instant, she considered refusing, only to admit that was impossible. What he offered— knowledge, ecstasy, fulfillment—was irresistible.

Her hand trembled only slightly as she placed it in his.

Chapter 9

THE SHEET WAS SMOOTH AND COOL BENEATH HER BACK. A soft breeze wafted through the open porthole, blowing gently over her heated skin.

The lights in the cabin were switched off; only the moon's silvery radiance shone on the man and woman entwined on the bed.

Cassia moaned, her head tossing back and forth on the pillows. She had no idea how long Tristan had been making love to her, but she knew that she was fast approaching the point where she would not be able to endure anything more.

A sheen of perspiration covered her skin. Her eyes were half closed, slumberous with passion. Her nostrils distended as she panted softly, breathing in the scents of full, unbridled arousal. Her lips parted, full and ripe, her tongue darting out to moisten them.

She arched her neck, her fingers digging into the mattress as yet another wave of ecstasy hit her.

It left her weak and stunned, yet by no means satisfied. She wanted . . . needed something she could not name.

Tristan raised his head, smiling down at her gently. "Easy, love, we're almost there." He dropped a tender kiss on her mouth, touching her breasts with feather-light caresses that only accentuated the throbbing ache of her nipples.

His eyes glittered with the fires of passion long held in check and soon to burst all bonds. Never would he have believed he could go so slowly with a woman and so completely subordinate his own needs to hers. Yet with Cassia, he found that everything was new and fresh to him.

He loved the soft cries she made, and the way her body moved beneath his. The touch, taste, and scent of her all delighted him.

He was enthralled by the ongoing transformation from shy, unaware girl to magnificently sensual woman. She was everything he had hoped for and more.

Not an inch of her lovely body had gone untouched by him. His hands and mouth had explored her from head to toe.

He had learned that the touch of a finger drawn along the sole of her foot made her toes curl under and wrung a helpless giggle from her. The backs of her knees and the insides of her elbows were equally susceptible, as were the hollows of her armpits and the undercurve of her breasts.

The feel of his tongue swirling around her nipples alternated with small, careful love bites made her cry out in delight. When he parted the folds of her womanhood with gentle fingers and caressed her there, her eyes grew smoky with pleasure. And when he bestowed the most intimate of kisses on her, the whole, slender length of her quivered in his arms.

As he had suspected, she was modest, but not prudish. Though much of what he did clearly startled her, she denied him nothing.

Her trust in him touched him deeply. He wanted to give her everything, to make her fully aware of her own capacity for pleasure and at the same time to so attune her to him that she would never be able to forget what they had shared.

When he turned her over and straddled her buttocks with his taut thighs, she stiffened momentarily. But the soft murmur of his voice in her ear and the gentle massaging of her shoulder blades was enough to ensure her acquiescence.

For Cassia, having him sit astride her was oddly unsettling, yet she could not find the will to protest. Somehow her inability to see Tristan increased her excitement all the more. She felt at once submissive to him and exultantly aware of her own power.

His long, hard fingers with their calloused tips moved down along the line of her spinal column, digging in gently to release the last vestiges of muscle tension. By the time he reached the curve of her bottom, she was almost limp.

He slid back slightly onto her upper thighs so that he could see her smooth, alabaster buttocks grasped in his big hands. Gently squeezing and kneading, he smiled at her sighs of pleasure.

A very male glint shone in his eyes as he decided that she was being just a little too complacent. Bending lower, he nipped at the soft fullness in his hands and laughed at her yelp of dismay.

"Tristan . . . !"

"I couldn't resist," he chuckled. "You're too delectable."

All well and good, Cassia thought dazedly, but it wouldn't do to let him get too much of the upper hand. Not quite sure what reaction she would get, she raised her buttocks slightly, allowing them to brush against his fully aroused manhood.

Tristan gasped, and his hands abruptly tightened on her. All his carefully contained passion surged to the fore. If she didn't stop, he was in danger of . . .

"Cassia," he growled, "don't do that."

Delighted by his reaction, she chose to ignore the warning. Instead, she continued the light, teasing motion of her lower body against his.

Looking at him over her shoulder, she murmured, "I don't want to stop. You've had your way long enough. It's my turn."

Such audacity from a virgin took his breath away. Before he could recover, she had wiggled out from under him and gently but firmly pushed him onto his back. He complied bemusedly, wondering what she intended to do now.

Cassia was wondering the same thing. She knew

nothing about how to make love to a man. Her only idea was to adapt his stunning exploration of her body to his own.

Sitting back on her heels, she studied him intently. His eyes were shuttered, his mouth taut. The skin over his high cheekbones was flushed, and the sinews of his neck and shoulders were corded with strain. His powerfully muscled arms were stretched out at his sides, the hands clenched.

As she watched, fascinated, the sheet of muscles covering his abdomen rippled spasmodically.

A quiver of anticipation pulsated through her. She stopped thinking, stopped wondering, and gave herself up to the simple pleasures of action.

Far in the back of her mind she understood what it cost him to lie quietly beneath her and allow her the freedom to taste and touch as she would. His patience filled her with tenderness and gave her the courage to explore him fully.

His burnished skin was faintly salty against her tongue. The line of hair trailing down his abdomen was like rough silk. She could feel the pounding of his heartbeat and knew that even his incredible control must shatter soon.

Before that happened she was determined to know all of him. Emboldened by his obvious delight, Cassia cupped the fullness of his manhood in her small hand and squeezed lightly.

When he groaned huskily she jumped, afraid that she might have hurt him, but realized quickly that whatever pain he suffered was only the male equivalent of what she herself had experienced.

More confident, she returned to her explorations, her attention now on that part of him that would soon be deep inside her.

Hardly aware that she spoke, she murmured, "How odd . . ."

Caught in the throes of passion, Tristan managed something that sounded like a laugh. Feeling his eyes on her, Cassia blushed and met his gaze hesitantly. "I meant the mechanics of it all," she explained, concerned that he would not understand and doubting her ability to make it any clearer.

He drew in a long, shaky breath and gently grasped her shoulders. "I know it's harder for you than for me, especially this first time. You have to let me into you, into your most private place. There is nothing more intimate."

As she nodded mutely, he brushed a finger along her smooth cheeks. "Believe me, it's all right. I'm not some . . . marauder who will hurt you. Only a man who wants to make you very happy."

Cassia did believe him. But she was glad all the same to know that he really understood how she felt.

Even as she acknowledged that his self-control had to be strained to the utmost, she realized that if he were rough or hurried at this point, all the trust being built up between them would be shattered.

But Tristan's patience seemed to be limitless. Drawing her gently down beside him, he soothed her with tender caresses until he was certain that his body would not betray him. Only then did he ease her onto her back.

"Don't be afraid," he murmured as he lowered

himself between her thighs. "You're completely ready for this. Just relax and trust me."

Cassia willingly did as he said. Her legs fell open to him as his hand delved gently to confirm her receptiveness. Only then did he move with stunning grace to give her the beginning of him.

The first touch of him within her made Cassia gasp, not because he felt strange, but because he did not. It was as though they had always been intended to fit together like this.

He hesitated, and her heart turned over. His own doubt and vulnerability washed away hers. With artless grace, she reached for him and guided him into her.

So thoroughly had he prepared her that the barrier of her virginity yielded easily. After an instant's resistance, he sank joyfully into the velvet sheath created for him alone.

Once there, he paused, letting them both become accustomed to each other. Propped up on his arms, he gazed down at her tenderly. "What a magnificent woman you are."

"You're not bad yourself," she murmured. Instinctively, she raised her legs twining them around his taut hips.

The unexpected movement, opening her farther to him, took Tristan by surprise. He was aware of the abrupt snapping of his long-tested restraint, and then he knew nothing except the need to find within her the fulfillment of all he was and yearned to be.

Cassia realized instantly that she had triggered something far beyond her expectations, but she welcomed it wholeheartedly. As he plunged deep inside her, she clasped him more tightly and moved to his driving rhythm.

With both so achingly aroused, culmination was only moments away. When it came, it was beyond anything Cassia could have imagined. She was transformed into a writhing flame that flared brighter and brighter against the darkness of oblivion.

Just as she thought she could not survive but was destined to be destroyed in the inferno, the flame shot higher still, carrying her with it into a place where all sense of herself vanished and there was only the peace of utter release.

In the next instant Tristan joined her, his hoarse cry smothered against her mouth. She felt his fulfillment as profoundly as she had her own, and knew at that moment a jolt of utter happiness so piercing as to bring tears to her eyes.

A long time later, when the aftershocks of ecstasy had stilled and they lay entwined in each other's arms, he looked down at her tenderly. His mouth curved in a gentle smile as he teased, "I think we've discovered another talent of yours, Cassia."

She had the grace to blush, but that did not prevent her from answering him saucily. "Don't give me all the credit. I was wonderfully inspired."

"I'm glad to hear it," he growled, gathering her even closer. As she cuddled against him, her head resting on his chest, he marveled at how different this experience was from any other he had ever known.

That a virgin could arouse him to such a crescendo

and bring him to so shattering a release was startling enough, but that was not the end of her surprises.

Always before, sexual satisfaction had left him feeling vaguely depressed and anxious to be gone. Only good manners had forced him to remain in bed with a woman after their mutual desires were satisfied.

Now he found that simply lying close to Cassia, holding her slender body in a passionless embrace, brought him a deep sense of contentment.

He valued that; any sane man would. But he also realized it could be dangerous.

A sexual relationship with her would never be enough by itself to satisfy him; he wanted far more. More, in fact, than she might be either willing or able to give.

Cassia murmured softly in his arms. Her eyes flickered closed and her body relaxed against him. As trustingly as a child, she drifted off to sleep.

As he gazed down at her, Tristan's mouth tightened as he considered the irony of his predicament.

All the mundane conventions he had once looked down on were returning with a vengeance. She made him think of things he had never even considered before: a future together, mutual commitment, perhaps even a family.

It was madness to indulge in such fantasies. He had always prided himself on being a hard-headed realist.

Pragmatically, chances were that he was simply a means to an end for her, a way of satisfying her quite natural curiosity. To expect anything would be to set himself up for severe disappointment.

He laughed humorlessly in the darkness. What did he want, hearts and flowers?

Here he was lying in bed with a magnificently beautiful woman with whom he had just shared a deeply satisfying sexual experience and would undoubtedly do so again. Yet he was complaining that that wasn't enough.

In today's world, casual sex was commonplace. He had indulged in it often enough himself to know that. What was to stop Cassia from doing the same?

A fierce sense of possessiveness rose up in him. His arms tightened around her. However little sense it made, he couldn't deny that the thought of her sharing such intimacies with another was unbearable.

She was his; he was the first man to enter the ivory tower that had sheltered her, and he meant to be the last.

It wasn't very modern or sophisticated, but he couldn't seem to care about that. Something very primitive was stirring within him, a savage need to claim his woman and keep her safe from all others.

His eyes narrowed in glittering resolve. Cassia might have some idea that she was free to indulge her newly awakened senses wherever she chose, but he intended to show her otherwise.

His lovemaking had gentled her to his hand; now he intended to tame her so completely that she would be helpless to deny him anything.

Chapter 10

TRISTAN WAS GONE BY THE TIME CASSIA AWOKE THE next morning. She had a dim memory of him slipping from the bunk before dawn. He had kissed her tenderly and whispered that he was going to his cabin to shower and change.

Much as she hated to see him go, she appreciated his discretion. The days ahead would be difficult enough without letting their personal relationship complicate things further.

Stretching languorously, she smiled to herself. The world was different this morning. She was far more vividly aware of everything around her, and most particularly of her body.

Never had she felt so utterly relaxed. The mere thought of moving seemed too much. Yet she could not deny her eagerness to see Tristan again. Even though they would have to be circumspect in their behavior, simply being near him would make the day even lovelier and brighter.

After leaving the bunk, she strolled into the small bathroom and turned on the shower. Standing under it, she gazed down at herself, wondering if the changes in her were as visible as they seemed.

Her skin was smoother and more radiant than ever before. Her breasts seemed fuller, the nipples still partially aroused. She soaped herself slowly, vividly remembering the feel of Tristan's hands and mouth moving over her.

A slow blush seeped across her cheeks and down the slender line of her throat as she thought of the things that had passed between them in the night. Never would she have believed herself capable of such wholehearted wantonness. With him, she had found a sense of freedom made all the more precious by its rarity.

She turned off the water and reached for a towel, puzzling over how anyone could share such shattering intimacies indiscriminately. Could it be that what she had experienced last night went beyond the ordinary bounds of lovemaking?

That must be it, she thought smilingly, otherwise men and women would always be in bed together and nothing else would ever get done.

As she slipped into a clean pair of jeans and a loose cotton shirt, Cassia thought wistfully how wonderful it would be if she and Tristan could just ignore the rest of the world and concentrate on each other. But that wasn't to be.

If everything went according to schedule, *Questor* would arrive that morning at the location worked out by Professor al-Bardi. Work would begin immediately to survey the site and decide the best approach to excavation.

All the members of the expedition would rightly be expected to give their best. Resolutely promising herself that she would not let her personal feelings shortchange her professional efforts, Cassia went up on deck.

A scene of ordered chaos greeted her. Crew members hurried back and forth checking the two-man sub that would be used for the initial explorations, preparing the underwater cameras, and studying the ultrasensitive instruments that tracked temperature, wind, and other weather indicators.

Stepping carefully to avoid coils of cable, she found a relatively quiet spot at the stern where she could watch without being in the way. Jason Lombard was already there, puffing on his pipe and studying the preparations with keen interest.

"Good morning," he greeted her with a perceptive glance. "I hope you slept well?"

Cassia managed to nod calmly. "Very, and you?"

"I tossed and turned a bit," the archaeologist admitted. Wryly, he added, "I'm always like a kid at the start of an expedition. And with this one in particular, it's hard to contain my excitement."

"That's understandable." She smiled sympathetically. "If I really let myself think about what may be down there, I'd be tempted to dive right in and start looking."

Jason laughed and leaned back against the railing. "Our esteemed leader wouldn't go for that. Tristan runs a tight ship."

At the mention of him, Cassia's pulse leaped. She struggled to remain composed, but could not completely prevent a slight tremor in her voice as she asked, "Speaking of whom, have you seen him around this morning?"

"He's in the pilothouse," Jason said, indicating the on-deck cabin that held the ship's main controls. "Nobody can handle *Questor* as well as Tristan. Understandably, since he designed her. So he'll be positioning us above the site himself."

Shielding her eyes, Cassia looked toward the plate-glass window. Tristan stood in clear view. Dressed as usual in a khaki shirt and slacks, he stood with easy grace beside the instrument panel.

His burnished skin emphasized the rugged masculinity of his features. Even at this early hour, his dark red hair was already somewhat tousled. The hard lines of his face were more relaxed than usual, and he seemed to be in a good humor.

Oblivious to all else, she stared at him intently. He spoke to someone nearby, and the simple movement of his lips fascinated her. When he raised a hand to adjust an overhead lever, a tremor raced through her.

All too vividly she remembered the feel of those

same lips, that same hand, moving over her body, commanding it to blinding ecstasy.

Abruptly aware that Jason was observing her curiously, Cassia smothered a sigh. Somehow she had to distract herself before her thoughts became obvious to all.

Turning her back on the pilothouse, she said, "Tell me what you think we will find down there."

The archaeologist smiled before he said, "Perhaps nothing. You certainly know as well as I how chancy this is. But should we succeed . . ."

"Yes, then what will we find?"

Her eagerness made him chuckle. "Nothing that looks very dramatic, I'm afraid. No golden crowns or diamond-studded scepters. Should we manage to turn up any evidence at all of human activity here, I will be delighted. If we stumble across so much as a single artifact with the tiniest bit of writing on it, I'll be ecstatic."

"It doesn't sound," Cassia said wryly, "as though you think I'll have much to do."

He shrugged philosophically. "The sea can be very stingy with what she gives back to us. But when she does preserve something, it tends to be in far better condition than anything we can find on land."

"Why is that?"

"The combination of cool underwater temperatures and the lack of oxygen necessary for decay mean that any artifact that survives whatever event placed it in the sea to begin with has a fairly good chance of enduring for centuries."

"What about the currents?" she asked. "Don't they eventually destroy everything that gets in their way?"

"Certainly a great deal is lost like that. But whatever manages to sink into the silt on the floor of the ocean is protected from just about all natural forces that might destroy it."

Cassia stared down at the blue-green water pensively, wondering what mysteries it might reveal. Even if the papyrus were correct, after so long could they really hope to find traces of a lost civilization?

"You said centuries," she reminded him quietly, "but if Atlantis existed at all, it was thousands of years ago."

"True, and that makes our task all the more difficult. But still not impossible." Jason's wise eyes gleamed. "Especially not given Tristan's tenacity. Once he makes up his mind, nothing gets in his way."

Resisting the impulse to look in his direction again, she asked, "You respect him greatly, don't you?"

"Respect and admire. He's triumphed over enormous odds to achieve more than most men can even dream of."

Cassia listened to him in fascination. Anything and everything to do with Tristan enthralled her. She could have happily spent all day hearing whatever the archaeologist could tell her about him, but there were other things to do.

While they had been talking, *Questor* had been moving in an ever-tightening circle. Now the powerful engines slowed, coming gradually to rest, and the anchor chain was let down.

In the sudden silence that followed, Cassia instinctively glanced toward the pilothouse. She wanted to share the moment with Tristan and was gratified to discover that, despite all that was going on around him, his eyes had already sought her out.

Their gazes met, hers warm and caressing despite all her resolve, his . . . She hesitated, thinking she must be mistaken. Surely he was not really looking at her so coldly, as if she had somehow done something to anger him?

Thinking she must be mistaken, she shot him a tentative smile. His only response was a deepened frown.

A wave of bleakness washed over her. The beauty of the day faded perceptibly. Confronted by his inexplicably hostile mood, she was forced to consider the possibility that he might regret what had happened between them.

Her stomach clenched painfully as she jerked her eyes away. In place of blissful contentment came dread. Had she, despite all her care, still managed to make a terrible mistake?

Jason had been watching the silent encounter and understood it all too well. Memories of his own turbulent youth returned as he contemplated the pair before him. Gently, he asked, "Is something wrong?"

"No," Cassia said too quickly. Her hands clenched on the deck railing so tightly that the knuckles turned white.

Hard on her surprise and disappointment came anger. What right did Tristan have to look at her like that, to spoil in any way the beauty of what they had shared?

Her blue-gray eyes, which a moment before had been clouded with concern, hardened. She might have been knocked for a loop by his sensual expertise, but she was still an intelligent woman with spirit and backbone.

Not for the world would she let him treat her like this. If Tristan thought he was going to get away with it, he was in for quite a shock.

Aware that Jason was still studying her, Cassia took a deep breath and forced herself to behave calmly. "I was just thinking of something I'd better take care of."

He nodded, although she could see he was not fooled. Hastily, she excused herself and headed below deck, where she hoped to gather her scattered wits and plan some way of coping with this unexpected turn of events.

Unfortunately, the lab did not offer the seclusion she had hoped. To begin with, Veda was there, eager to chat about information she'd turned up about earlier searches for Atlantis.

Cassia listened to her distractedly. The intellectual objectivity she had so long taken for granted was gone. All she could think about was Tristan and the pain he made her feel.

When Veda at last broke off, Cassia barely noticed. She didn't see the little computer blink sympathetically. In her mind's eye, all she saw was the man who had roused her to such passion the night before and whose seemingly abrupt turnaround she could not begin to understand.

She was sitting at the worktable with her chin leaning heavily on the palm of her hand when the door opened behind her. The sound made her breath catch in her throat. She took a firm grip on herself and turned to face Tristan.

But she discovered that it was not him but Hank who had sought her out.

"I noticed you weren't on deck," he explained cheerfully, "and since we're about to launch the submersible, I thought I'd come and get you. You don't want to miss this."

Managing a weak smile that she hoped hid both her relief and her disappointment, Cassia slid off her stool. "You're right; I don't."

"Great." Hank held the door open for her as she preceded him out into the corridor. Together they went up on deck. He was eagerly telling her all about how the small sub worked as they emerged into the sunshine.

Despite herself, she couldn't help but be interested. The sub was a miracle of miniaturization that made use of some of the same technology she had built into Veda.

Though its computers were nowhere near as sophisticated, they were capable of plotting a course to depths of five thousand feet and keeping the crew safe at temperatures and pressures where all but the most elementary life was impossible.

Sean Garrison was standing beside the sub, having

just completed his last predive check. When he saw
Cassia, he waved her over. "Really something, isn't
she?"

"I'll say. Are you going down in her?"

He nodded. "Wouldn't miss it for the world. All
the fun of diving without the work."

His offhand dismissal of the difficulties involved in
such a venture didn't fool her for a moment. Controlling the sub required not only technical skill but
also superb reflexes. Few men could have handled
the job.

"Somehow I think it's more difficult than you
say," she demurred gently.

"Not for us," Hank insisted. "We just sit back and
let Tristan do all the work. He built her, so he has to
run her."

"Are we using anything he didn't invent?" Cassia
inquired glumly. His presence was inescapable
enough without her being constantly reminded of
him.

Sean thought for a moment, then shook his head.
"Maybe one or two little things, but not more than
that. This expedition is all his. Nobody else could
have put it together."

He spoke so admiringly that Cassia sighed. It was
on the tip of her tongue to say something, anything,
that would change the subject when she abruptly
became aware that she was being watched.

Without turning her head, she knew that Tristan
was looking at her. His formidable scrutiny pierced
the facade of her self-possession and made her feel
frighteningly vulnerable.

If she turned in his direction, would she see him glowering at her as he had before? She couldn't bear to confront that again, but neither was she willing to let him see how he affected her.

Instead she drew on instincts only recently stirred to life and gave Sean her most dazzling smile. "It's all so fascinating. Do you think I could see the inside?"

Startled by her unexpected warmth, which breached the barriers of mere professionalism, he nonetheless managed to recover swiftly. "Sure thing. Here, let me give you a boost up."

His hands round her waist were warm and strong as he lifted her effortlessly toward the hatch leading inside the sub.

Hank, observing the scene, was not willing to be left out. He reached up to steady her with a hand at the small of her back.

With such gallant assistance, Cassia made it down the ladder leading to the interior of the sub. Once inside, she studied her surroundings curiously.

The compartment was very small and low-ceilinged. She had to crouch to keep her head clear of the metal roof. There was almost no room to maneuver, but with care she managed to squeeze out of the way as Hank and Sean joined her.

"Have a seat," Sean said, gesturing to one of the two leather-padded chairs in front of the control console. "I'll explain how this lovely thing works."

Cassia did as he suggested. In front of her were banks of instruments that controlled speed, direction, and depth, as well as inside temperature, pressure, and the exact mix of gases the crew would breath.

Above them was a wide expanse of concave window forming the nose of the sub. Once they were below the surface, it would provide a stunning view of the undersea surroundings.

To her right was another console that operated the underwater cameras. To the left a powerful radio provided communication with the surface.

As Sean pointed out the remarkable features of the vehicle, Hank draped himself over Cassia's chair. One large hand rested lightly on her shoulder in a gesture that was no more than friendly.

She wasn't at all disturbed by it. Since her first encounter with Hank, he had given every indication of having accepted her refusal to mix business with pleasure.

Remembering how she had broken that rule with Tristan, Cassia flushed. She was paying a heavy price for her hypocrisy.

Distracted by her thoughts, she was unaware when Sean abruptly broke off his explanations and turned toward the hatch. Not until he rose and headed in that direction did she realize that something was wrong.

From above, a deep voice ordered, "What the hell do you think you're doing, Garrison?"

Sean's mouth tightened, but he answered calmly. "Just giving Cassia a tour of the sub, Tristan. I didn't think you'd mind."

"You thought wrong. Get out. All three of you."

Hank and Sean exchanged surprised glances, but

didn't argue. They agilely lifted themselves through the hatch, then bent down to help Cassia. Before they could do so, Tristan snapped, "Never mind about that. You're both needed in the pilothouse."

In the face of such a clear dismissal, there was nothing either man could do except shoot her an apologetic look. She was left to pull herself through the narrow opening without assistance.

Tristan had climbed down the outside ladder of the sub and was waiting for her on deck. He scowled darkly. "I told you to behave yourself around the men."

Cassia stared at him, dumbfounded. The sheer injustice of it astounded her. Her hands balled into fists at her sides as she glared at him. Coldly, she said, "I won't even dignify that with a response. If and when you decide to try acting like an adult, let me know." Turning her back on him before he could see the anguish in her eyes, she deliberately walked away.

A dull flush darkened his high-boned cheeks. It was all he could do not to reach out and stop her. But he sensed what an explosion that would trigger and thought it prudent not to have any witnesses.

It would be far wiser to talk elsewhere, but with the sub about to be launched, he was needed on deck. All too aware of the lovely sight she made with her back held proudly straight and her softly rounded bottom swaying slightly, he stifled the urge to forget his responsibilities and sweep her into his arms right then and there.

That was undoubtedly what Errol Flynn would do.

But then, he hadn't had to contend with a spitting termagant who looked as though she would be only too happy to see him vanish right off the face of the earth.

Tristan had never thought himself inept when it came to handling women. On the contrary, he had always enjoyed notable success in that area. But Cassia threw him. With her his instinctive defensiveness, his self-control, and even his common sense all went out the window.

Sighing, he shook his head resignedly. He hadn't set out to make her angry, but somehow he had succeeded just the same. Moreover, he suspected he had also hurt her.

Ruefully, he reminded himself that she was a sensitive, temperamental filly who needed careful controlling. Hadn't he proved just the night before how well she responded to a gentle hand?

If he'd done it once, he could no doubt do it again. That thought cheered him and allowed him to turn his thoughts back to the sub-launching with an easy spirit.

Had he been able to see into Cassia's thoughts at that moment, he would have felt anything but confident. She was feeling none too charitable toward the male sex in general and Tristan in particular.

And her determination to teach him a well-deserved lesson had redoubled.

Chapter 11

THERE WAS LITTLE CONSOLATION FOR CASSIA IN THE knowledge that Tristan would be too preoccupied the rest of the day to upset her further. He had already succeeded in infuriating her and had made it all but impossible for her to concentrate on anything but him.

Although she went through the motions of studying the reports prepared by Veda regarding the types of artifacts they might hope to find, her mind was firmly elsewhere. Again and again she found excuses to go on deck and see how the submersible was doing.

After some three hours below the surface, Tristan and Sean had mapped out the entire site and photographed it in square-yard sections. Now began the nerve-racking work of discovering whether or not there was anything of interest to investigate further.

An air of tense anticipation hung over the ship as the little sub was hoisted out of the water and carefully deposited back on board. Cassia was watching from the sidelines when Tristan and Sean pulled themselves through the narrow hatch and climbed down the ladder to *Questor*'s gently rocking deck.

Sean's usual smile was gone; he looked every inch the serious professional. But nonetheless it was obvious that he was buoyed up by the experience.

"It's incredible down there," he said in response to inquiries from the rest of the crew. "The water is crystal clear to several hundred feet, and there's no evidence of any disturbances, not recent ones, at any rate."

"Then you think we've got a shot at it?" Hank asked eagerly.

Before Sean could reply, Tristan raised a hand. To Cassia's perceptive gaze, he looked tired and under considerable strain. She had to stifle the urge to go to him. Only the memory of his recent treatment of her kept her from obeying the instinct to offer comfort.

His gaze flicked to her for a moment before he told the crew, "It's too early to say what we've got. You'll all have a chance to take a look at the photos and tell me what you think, but in the meantime let's get back to work."

They obeyed him readily, each man returning to his duties. Cassia wished she could muster such self-discipline. Feeling unaccountably at loose ends, she loitered on deck for a short time before deciding there was no good reason why she shouldn't go down to the lab and see how things were going.

She arrived in time to find Jason helping Tristan to load the film into the developer. The archaeologist greeted her with a smile. "Come over here and hold this, would you?" he asked, indicating one of the strips of exposed film. "We seem to be short a pair of hands."

Doing as he said, she glanced at Tristan. Their gazes locked, hers wary and defensive, his guarded, revealing none of his thoughts.

After the night they had spent together, any rift between them was unbearable to Cassia. Her throat was tight and her eyes burned as she looked away, determined not to let him see how much he had hurt her.

If Jason sensed the undercurrents of their silent exchange, he gave no sign. Instead he patiently continued feeding film into the developer and re-checking the exposure times to be sure they would get the clearest possible prints.

When the photos began to emerge for drying, Cassia could not help but feel disappointed. They seemed to be no more than pretty underwater scenes showing the usual assortment of coral, sea plants, and fish.

Sensing her letdown, Tristan said, "Don't jump to any conclusions until we've gone over these thoroughly. Appearances can be deceptive."

Under ordinary circumstances, she would have

found nothing in that remark in the least offensive.
But with all her defenses bristling, Cassia thought it
sounded patronizing. He seemed to be talking to her
as though she were an impulsive child instead of an
experienced scholar.

"I'm well aware of the need for further study,"
she snapped. "You might remember that I've had
more than a little experience with research projects
at least as complicated as this one."

Tristan's mouth hardened at her censorious tone.
Last night she had been so sweetly yielding in his
arms; now she seemed to be singing a completely
different song.

In place of the delightful seductress who had
effortlessly enchanted him was a suspicious, angry
critic who appeared determined to misconstrue
everything he said and did.

Grimly, he told himself that he was not about to
stand still for that. As soon as circumstances permit-
ted, they were going to have it out. Whatever bee
she had gotten in her bonnet, he intended to make it
crystal clear to her who called the shots in their
relationship.

Having so resolved, he turned his attention back
to the rapidly drying prints. "Let's take these to the
galley so everyone can get a look at them."

Careful not to smudge any, the three of them
carried the photos down the corridor and spread
them out on the large table. As the rest of the
members of the expedition gathered around eagerly,
Tristan explained what needed to be done.

"What you want to be looking for are anomalies,

breaks in the natural order, anything that might indicate a human presence, however remote in time. That could be something as simple as rust stains that might indicate the presence of coins or chains, or a depression in the sand that could mean a structure of some sort once stood there. Take your time and don't expect too much right off the bat."

Silence settled over the table, punctuated only by the rustle of photos being passed around and the occasional murmurs of the men as they thought they might have spotted something, only to decide a moment later that they had not.

It was slow going and very frustrating. Before very long, Hank muttered, "Talk about looking for a needle in a haystack. I don't see a thing."

"Maybe you're expecting too much," Jason suggested quietly. "Put any ideas you've got about ruined temples and the like out of your mind. When we find it, whatever *it* is, it's going to be so nondescript as to be barely noticeable."

Cassia knew what he meant. Although she had never been involved in anything exactly like this, all her experience indicated that progress was most often made in tiny, almost indiscernible steps, not the huge leaps most people imagined.

She had long ago learned to approach such tasks without preconceived notions, to open herself to all possibilities. A good example was the close-up of the rock she was studying. Lying partially covered by shifting sand, it had an unusually flat top with indentations on it that to the perceptive eye resembled the marks of a long-ago chisel.

Of course, there could be many other explanations for what she was seeing: the ordinary motion of water over the eons, for instance. Yet some small, barely formed sense of excitement caused her to reach for the next photo, a wider scan shot of the same location.

Next to the rock lay another of similar size and marking. There was a gap of a foot or two, then a scattering of rocks that looked as though they might have tumbled from some higher spot.

Reminding herself that she was hardly an expert in this field, and that she might well be looking at a perfectly explainable natural phenomenon, Cassia nonetheless pursued her effort to locate the source of the rocks.

She found it after a dozen or so photos, when her eyes lit on a long, low bulge in the flat surface of the seafloor. About ten feet long and three feet in height all along its length, the rise was covered with lichen and other sea growth.

But when she looked very closely, she could see glimpses of rocks similar to those lying nearby.

Hesitation gripped her as she considered the implications of what she had found. Ordinarily she wouldn't have hesitated to suggest a theory, even a rather farfetched one, and let her colleagues make of it what they would.

The possibility that she might be wrong did not faze her. But the fear that Tristan would deride her did.

Already he had shown a regrettable tendency to treat her like a child rather than a professional. She loathed the idea of giving him yet another opportunity to do so.

A compromise suggested itself; Jason sat directly across the table from her, puffing on his unlit pipe as he poured over the photos intently. Tristan was beside him, talking quietly with Sean. The other men seemed equally distracted.

As unobtrusively as she could, Cassia slid the photos toward the archaeologist. So engrossed was he in the series he was studying that he did not notice them at first.

Then they caught his eye, and to her dismay he said quite clearly, "Want me to look at these, do you? All right."

Cassia swallowed a groan as attention abruptly centered on her. She refused to look in Tristan's direction, instead picking up another group of photos and pretending to scrutinize them.

Scant seconds ticked by before Jason let out a low whistle. "It looks as though our Cassia has hit on something. Here, Tristan, what do you make of this?"

"Igneous rocks . . . basalt, probably. Unusually regular in shape and size . . . almost as though they had been—" He broke off, his gaze shifting to Cassia.

A bit grudgingly, to her ears at least, he said, "You're very perceptive. This isn't a natural formation."

That was all the other men needed to hear. They let loose with a barrage of eager questions. "All I can tell you," Tristan explained in response, "is that

Cassia appears to have located a wall. There's no indication yet of when it was constructed, or by whom. We'll have to take a much closer look."

"A wall means human beings have definitely been here, right?" Hank asked. His eyes were alight with anticipation shared, if to a more subdued degree, by everyone at the table.

"Unless dolphins have taken to construction," Tristan laughed, "that's exactly what it means. But remember, any number of people have been through this area. We can't jump to any conclusions about who's responsible for this."

With the enviable ebullience of youth, Hank shrugged that off. "It had to be the Atlantans who did it. Who else could have built a wall under water?"

At the laughter that greeted this, he blushed but showed no resentment. "Okay, so I'm missing something. Explain it to me."

Jason took his pipe out of his mouth and assumed his best professorial manner. "Underwater construction is extremely difficult; even with all our technology it's very dangerous and expensive. Therefore, the presence of a wall indicates that at some time this area was above water."

"That's the clearest indication we could have that we've found the location described in the papyrus," Tristan added, "since the Atlantis legend rests on the existence of a civilization that was destroyed when its island nation sank beneath the waves."

The men nodded their understanding and did not hesitate to praise Cassia for the discovery. Tristan's response to this was a sardonic watchfulness that quickly discomfited her.

She was relieved when it came time for dinner and the photos had to be put away. Throughout the meal, which for all its excellence she barely tasted, she was acutely aware of him.

He dominated her senses as easily as he filled her thoughts. She was powerless to block him out, no matter how resentful or angry she might be.

The long day everyone had put in led inevitably to an early end to the evening. Cassia slipped away gratefully, looking forward to the privacy of her cabin, where she could confront her uneasy thoughts and try to make some sense of them.

But that was not to be. Barely had she showered and slipped into a thin cotton nightie than there was a knock at the door.

She had no doubt who stood on the other side. Giving in to a wave of cynicism, she told herself that after the night they had shared it was only natural for Tristan to come looking for more.

Resolved that he was going to be sorely disappointed, she answered his knock. His eyes moved over her heatedly as he stepped into the small cabin, but his tone was chilling. "You shouldn't open the door like that. What if it hadn't been me?"

Cassia shrugged disparagingly. For all her good intentions, she was hardly immune to the impact of his nearness.

In deference to the warm night air, his khaki shirt hung open, baring the full expanse of his lean chest. All too vividly she remembered the feel of his burnished skin against her own.

A treacherous weakness seeped through her, prompting a sharp retort. "What if it hadn't? I'm sure every man on this ship knows what a woman looks like."

Sea-green eyes glinted angrily. "That's hardly a reason to be so careless. You give them enough to look at as it is."

A bitter sense of vindication swept through Cassia. She had been right to be angry at him. He was every bit as arrogant and insufferable as she had feared.

"I see no reason to be insulted in my own cabin. Kindly leave."

The look he gave her would have been humorous, under different circumstances. For whatever it was worth, she had managed to surprise him.

Disbelievingly, he insisted, "You don't mean that."

"I most certainly do! From the moment I came on deck this morning you were cold and contemptuous. You treated me as though I were some kind of criminal."

"That's ridiculous! You're supposed to be an intelligent woman. How do you manage to come up with such crackpot notions?"

"I am an intelligent woman! But you seem determined to treat me like a not very bright child."

"Oh, really? And I suppose what happened last night was treating you like a child?"

At the mention of what they had shared such a short time before, Cassia began to tremble. What an incredible difference a few hours could make. The cabin that had been the setting of joyful love-making was now the scene of acrimony and resentment.

Huskily, she murmured, "How could you be so insensitive as to bring that up? Don't you care at all for my feelings?"

"Of course I do." Grudgingly, he added, "But I sure don't seem to understand them. What have I done to upset you like this?"

"Besides making me feel like a pariah? That little scene with Hank and Sean made it clear you don't have even the rudiments of professional respect for me. How am I supposed to work with the men under those conditions?"

Despite himself, Tristan had to admit that she had a point. He had let his personal feelings for her get in the way of their working relationship. But, damn it, didn't she understand that he was so thrown by what was happening between them that he could barely think straight?

"Cassia . . . I admit there's some justification for what you're saying. But I think you're only looking at this from one point of view—your own. Have you considered how I feel?"

That brought her up short. It was true that throughout that long, painful day she had been completely absorbed with nurturing her own hurt and resentment. Had she missed something she should not have?

Meeting his eyes, she saw his doubt and anguish clearly for the first time. Her throat tightened as a flicker of hope darted through her. "I guess I have been self-centered . . . maybe because I'm afraid to know how you feel."

His face softened. Wryly, he said, "That makes two of us. You scare the daylights out of me."

Cassia could not hide her surprise. She was beyond even trying. It had never so much as occurred to her that he might still have his own fears about their relationship.

Grimly, she considered that her lack of perception didn't say anything good about her. She hadn't completely left the ivory tower after all.

Part of her was still sealed in there, oblivious to everything except the narrow sliver of the world she saw through the window of her own concerns.

"I'm sorry . . ." she murmured. "I didn't realize . . ."

He took a step toward her. "I guess we've both got things to learn."

"Do you think we'll . . . be able to?"

Tristan looked at her intently. He made no attempt to minimize her question. Instead he said, "We're both supposed to be pretty smart."

"Maybe too smart for our own good."

"That's a possibility. All we can do is try."

Cassia nodded slowly, well aware that she was committing herself to a course of action that in many ways was far more serious and risky than the step she had taken the night before.

Then she had shared her body; now she would have to share both her heart and mind.

All that made it worth the attempt was that Tristan would have to do the same.

Chapter 12

NEVER IN CASSIA'S LIFE HAD TIME PASSED AS SWIFTLY as it did in the next few days. She had the constant sense of something rare and precious slipping away from her and of always struggling to hold on to it, to make each moment all that it could be.

With the new understanding between her and Tristan, the passion that had flared between them from the beginning reached unparalleled heights. Each night they lay entwined in her bunk, sharing the ultimate in sensual delights.

Each day they parted before the rest of the crew began to stir, he to return to his cabin, she to lie awake staring at the ceiling and remembering the hours just past.

At breakfast they met again, with their professional facades firmly in place. In public, they were polite and cooperative with each other, nothing more. The strain of hiding their feelings lent an almost intolerable tension to each day, making what happened between them at night all the more explosive.

Cassia did not flatter herself that their act fooled everyone. She suspected that Jason saw through it, and perhaps also Sean. Neither man said anything, but occasionally she glimpsed the faintest suggestion of a grin when one or the other of them happened to glance at her and Tristan.

On the sixth morning of the expedition, she rose even earlier than usual. Tristan had left her a short time before, and the touch of the sheets still warm from their lovemaking made her ache for his return.

Knowing that could not be, she showered and dressed, then went up on deck. The swollen red disk of the sun was just rising out of the indigo waters. Wisps of morning haze drifted over the sea.

Far in the distance she could make out the shape of a cruise ship heading for port. The contrail of a jet cleaved the cloudless sky miles above her head.

With the exception of those few reminders of the civilization they had left far behind, she might have been in a different world. All around her the advanced technology of *Questor* spoke of the future, while below the gently lapping waves the centuries were being peeled away to reveal the past.

Jason joined her as she leaned against the railing. With each day the archaeologist seemed to shed years. Now deeply tanned, with a perpetually excited gleam in his eyes, he looked almost like a young man embarked on a great adventure.

"Good morning, my dear," he greeted her. "Another lovely day, I see."

She smiled at his obvious contentment with that state of affairs. "Would it dare to be otherwise, with you constantly on guard for the slightest change in the weather?"

"I suppose I do check the instruments fairly often," he admitted, "but that's just because I can hardly believe our good fortune. So far, at least, this expedition is remarkably trouble free."

"Don't jinx us!" she teased. "Finding the wall this early on was incredible enough. We don't want to press our luck."

Jason raised an eyebrow at her in mock surprise. "Do you mean to tell me that a young lady of your intelligence and abilities actually believes in the vagaries of fate?"

Cassia turned away from him to stare out over the water. She was silent for several moments before she said, "Fate exists; it must. How else can anyone explain the sudden twists and turns our lives take?"

"I've often wondered that myself," the archaeologist said quietly as he tapped down the tobacco in his pipe. "We can go along for years more or less content, never realizing that we're working ourselves into a rut. Then quite suddenly something will happen to jar us out of it and make us consider possibilities we've never thought of before."

His words seemed to carry a special message for Cassia. Whether or not Jason realized it—and she suspected more strongly than ever that he did—her relationship with Tristan had brought her to a major crossroads in her life.

No matter what happened by the end of the expedition, she could never go back to the way she had been. Part of her regretted that, with a wistful nostalgia for the protection of innocence.

But that was more than equaled by the liberating sense of herself as a woman. As she had so many times in recent days, she told herself that come what might, she would have no regrets.

"Are you coming down with us today?" Jason asked, gently breaking in on her thoughts.

"What . . . ? Oh, yes, I am." She grinned wryly. "Sean says I'm turning into a fairly respectable diver."

"I believe what he said was that you had a natural ability for underwater work."

That was true; Sean had found her a remarkably apt pupil. But despite her easy adaptation to the submarine environment, Tristan had still been hesitant about letting her dive. Only when she had made it clear that she would regard it as a slight to her professionalism to be left behind had he reluctantly agreed.

An hour later, as Hank was helping her into her breathing equipment, Cassia felt Tristan's eyes on her. In the midst of fastening the strap that held the oxygen tanks in place, she looked up.

He was standing only a few feet away, also preparing to make the dive. Like the rest of the men, he wore only swimming briefs. His tall, superbly conditioned body glowed in the sun.

Unbidden, thoughts of the previous night rose to cloud Cassia's mind. With almost painful clarity she remembered the springiness of the hair covering his chest, the rough-silk texture of his hands with their skilled fingers that could strip her of all restraint, and the strength of his arms trembling slightly as he held himself above her in the midst of the ultimate act of love.

"Penny for 'em," Hank said cheerfully.

Cassia grimaced, abruptly yanked back to reality. She couldn't go on like this. First with Jason and now with Hank. Her preoccupation was bound to be noticed soon and to arouse curiosity.

Ignoring the perceptive grin Tristan shot her, she muttered, "You'd be wasting your money."

Hank shrugged and settled the tanks more comfortably on her back. "All set?"

As Sean had trained her to do, Cassia checked each buckle and valve once more before nodding. "All set. Your turn."

Since she had first started diving, she and Hank had worked together as a team. Sean insisted on the "buddy system." No diver ever went down alone, or into a remote area without someone else along. That was an absolutely unbendable rule, violation of which would bring instant dismissal from the crew.

Not that any of the divers would ever be foolish enough to break it. They all understood how quickly and unexpectedly something could go wrong underwater. The work was risky enough without adding needless dangers by going it alone.

With Hank's air equipment in place, they lowered

themselves into the ocean and, treading water, slipped on their flippers. Their masks were lowered and mouthpieces in place by the time Sean and Tristan joined them with the two other divers working that shift.

As had been decided earlier, the objective of the dive was to continue clearing the area around the wall. So far some thirty feet of its length had been cleared to a depth of ten feet.

That was accomplished by using *Questor*'s dredging arm to cut wide swathes through the sand. Jason had winced at this, as any good archaeologist would. He much preferred the meticulous whisk-broom-and-magnifying-glass technique that ran no risk of missing anything. But that was hardly practical under the circumstances.

Going on the fact that there was no indication of any historical importance to the site within the last several centuries, and calculating the rate of deposit of the seabed, Tristan was able to determine that cutting through ten feet would not cost them anything significant. At worst they might lose scattered remains of one of the numerous shipwrecks that had occurred over the centuries in the area.

Swimming along beside the wall, Cassia could fully appreciate the care and skill that had gone into its construction. The topmost portion, the part seen in the photo, was badly weathered. But the farther down they went, the longer the stones had been protected, and the more impressive they were.

Ten feet down it could be seen that the basalt fragments were all of almost exactly the same size and shape, and so perfectly fitted together as to require no mortar.

Only once before had she seen similar stonework, in the ruins of the Incas' great city of Machu Picchu. It did not escape her that the Inca had traded with the Aztecs, and had absorbed some of that great race's culture into their own.

The crystalline water shot through by broken rays of sunlight made it possible to see in great detail. As she had learned to do, Cassia swam slowly, studying the sandy bottom immediately beneath her.

Several times she stopped to examine pieces of debris. Each looked promising to begin with, but they all turned out to be bits of shell or stone, nothing to indicate who might have built the wall.

Up ahead she could see Tristan. The play of light and shadow over his body and the agile grace with which he moved made him seem like some otherworldly creature of the sea, perhaps a god of the waves come to life.

Smiling at her own flight of fancy, she forced her attention back to more mundane matters. Beside her, Hank paused to check his watch. He held up both hands, flashing ten fingers twice to indicate they had twenty minutes left.

She nodded and went on with her work, not really hoping to find anything, but still not willing to give up until the last possible moment.

For days now they had followed the same course, as each successive foot of sand was removed, trying to find some indication that they had dug deeply enough. Once again they seemed destined for disappointment.

Half an hour later she stood on deck, her breathing equipment removed, and briskly dried herself as she listened to Tristan and Sean talk over the dive.

"We struck out again," he explained to Jason, who had been waiting as anxiously as ever for the results. "There's absolutely nothing of interest except the wall itself. It looks to me as though we'll have to dredge at least another foot."

"At this rate," Sean said, "we could spend months peeling away layer by layer and still not find anything."

"Reluctantly, I'm inclined to agree with that," Jason admitted. "Perhaps more drastic measures are called for."

"If you're suggesting dredging more than a foot in one go," Tristan said, "I have to caution you that we have no way of knowing what we might destroy."

"There might be some method of determining that," Cassia suggested cautiously. She had been thinking about this problem of how much to dredge for several days and believed she might have hit on a solution.

"What we need is an equation that takes into account all events over the last forty-five hundred years that would have affected the rate of deposit of the seafloor. Using that, we should be able to determine how much has to be removed to bring us to the era of the papyrus."

"Wouldn't that be an extremely complex equation to develop?" Tristan asked dubiously.

"For any one of us, certainly. But not for Veda. She has immediate access to data banks describing every known change in tide and temperature, currents and wind, even earthquakes and volcanic eruptions. It's just a guess, but I think she might be able to come up with what we need within a matter of hours."

Jason was nodding eagerly, as was Sean. But Tristan looked unconvinced. "I know you want to help, but . . ."

Cassia's mouth tightened. She understood his caution, but it still seemed as though he was reluctant to afford her the same degree of professional respect he gave to every other member of the crew.

The passion they shared in the private hours of the night was blinding him to a side of her character completely apart from the warm, willing woman who trembled in his arms. Though her body had only just begun to come alive, her mind had always been that way. Nothing had happened to impair the keenness of her intelligence or the power of her reasoning.

"I'm not offering you any guarantees," she said softly, "but I think Veda may hold the key to this problem. All I'm asking is that we take the opportunity to find out."

She hadn't meant to sound so intent, almost as though she was pleading with him to give her the chance to prove herself. But that was the way the words came out.

Flushing, she had to tolerate his patient smile as he reluctantly agreed. "All right, give it a try. But don't get your hopes up too much. Some things are beyond even Veda's abilities."

Perhaps, but Cassia knew the computer's powers better than anyone. She had, after all, created her. It was on the tip of her tongue to remind him of that, but she decided not to.

They were walking a tightrope as it was, between their professional and personal needs. She didn't want to do anything to aggravate the situation if it could possibly be avoided.

But an hour later in the lab, as she watched Veda eagerly get to work on her new task, she remembered Tristan's reluctance and was hurt by it. Never before had she wanted anyone's approval as she did his.

The more she came to love him, the more she needed to know that there was true equality in their relationship. So long as he insisted on ignoring the full scope of her interests and abilities, there would be severe limits on what they could share.

A few days before she might have remonstrated with him about his limited view of her, but she had a much greater appreciation now of his own conflicts. Tristan was waging a battle within himself between the harsh lessons of a lifetime and the resurgent need to love.

On the one hand, he wanted to trust her completely. On the other, he was all too aware of how vulnerable that would make him. His solution, so far, seemed to be to accept the beguiling woman in her, but not necessarily the intelligent adult.

Throughout dinner, Cassia's mind kept coming

back to a single thought: If she and Tristan were to have any hope of a future together, they had to overcome the barriers of loneliness and doubt that threatened to drive them apart.

Listening with half an ear to the chatter of the crew, she wondered how that might be accomplished. Sheer sexual passion was certainly not enough. If anything, it might only be reinforcing Tristan's unwillingness to see her as more than a lovely creature to be possessed and protected.

Yet even knowing that, she could not turn him away when he came to her cabin that night. He found her seated on the bunk, wearing a silk caftan in delicate shades of mauve and blue. So fragile was the material that he could see she wore nothing beneath it.

His throat was tight as he shut the door behind him and locked it. For a moment he stood uncertainly, looking at her. He had blundered that afternoon when she offered Veda's help. His obvious doubts must have hurt her. Perhaps his presence was not welcome.

Cassia felt the wariness in him and was moved by it. Though it was still a shock to her to realize how vulnerable he could be, she was no longer at a loss as to how to deal with it.

Putting aside her own concerns, she rose gracefully and went to him.

Silk whispered around her bare feet and over her bare body. Her cheeks were slightly flushed, her eyes wide and luminous. Her moist lips parted as she breathed a bit raggedly.

Tristan watched her, at once entranced and wary. The last few days had brought home to him how powerless he was against her. In her he saw everything he had ever wanted and more that he had not even known how to dream of.

Yet a deeply rooted instinct for survival kept him from fully acknowledging that what had begun months before as simply physical desire had long since turned to heartfelt love.

He had come down to the cabin half expecting that they would argue. Then he could have stormed out and nursed his hurt in righteous vindication.

Tomorrow they would undoubtedly have made up, with all the pleasure that suggested. But they would essentially still be where they were now, with no need to confront the complexities of a deepening relationship.

Cassia was denying him that easy out. Instead of berating him as he suspected he deserved, she came to him as a beguiling seductress.

Even as he thought that, he corrected himself. No, she was something far simpler. And far more rare. A woman of strength and spirit and intelligence. A woman who cared enough for him to sometimes put his concerns ahead of her own.

The cracks in the wall around his heart widened. He sighed deeply, well aware that he was losing the battle to remain emotionally aloof—and not able to regret it in the least.

Chapter 13

TRISTAN LAY STRETCHED OUT ON THE BED, HIS TAUT skin glowing with a fine sheen of perspiration, and his powerful chest rising and falling urgently.

Cassia sat on her heels, regarding him intently. She was fascinated by his responses to her and made no secret of it.

Throughout the long hours of the night he had given her free rein to discover all that she would. She knew this was by way of apology for what had happened earlier, and didn't hesitate to take full advantage.

It was not as though she was harming him in any way. On the contrary, he could not have made it clearer that he delighted in her newfound boldness and skill.

Smiling gently, she shook her head as she considered the inherent contradictions of her own behavior. She who claimed to want to be treated as an adult and an equal did not hesitate to play the courtesan.

At least there was some satisfaction in the discovery that she was competent in the role.

"If you stop now," Tristan groaned huskily, "I can absolutely guarantee that my death will be on your head."

Cassia giggled softly, a most unlikely sound for her, but one that had been making its appearance lately with unavoidable regularity. Her gaze drifted to his manhood; his desire for her was obvious. "You look quite vigorous to me."

"That's true," he allowed with pardonable smugness. "But surely you wouldn't leave me in this condition."

She pretended to think that over. "It's been such a long day. I am rather tired. . . ."

"Oh, really . . ." Tristan reached out, his big hand cupping her breast, the thumb pressing lightly into her nipple. Without taking his eyes from hers, he began a leisurely, revolving motion that quickly dispelled her pretended lack of interest.

"You're right . . ." she murmured huskily. "It would be a shame to leave you like this." A hint of deviltry curved her mouth as she added, "After all, how would you get into your swimming trunks?"

"How indeed? Besides, what would happen if I bumped into something?"

"I can't bear to even think of that."

"Such a tender heart . . ." Distractedly, he

slipped his other hand between her thighs, fondling her gently where their lovemaking had already made her warm and moist.

A sigh rippled from her. Slowly, drawing out the anticipation, she lowered herself onto him.

At that first instant of intimate union, Tristan gasped. He was so acutely ready for her that he felt about to burst. Her body was a velvet sheath holding him in exquisite thrall.

In silent tribute to her womanhood, he forced himself to lie quiescent as Cassia set the pace for them. She went gradually, balancing on the very tip of him, caressing him with her hands and mouth until at last neither of them could bear any more.

Only then did she lower herself fully, taking him within herself with a powerful undulation that wrung a gasp from him. A heady sense of her own power washed through her as she began the pounding rhythm that would swiftly drain them both of strength.

They were on the edge of release when she paused, drawing herself upward again. Tristan instinctively tried to stop her, his big hands grasping her hips. But in his dazed state she was too quick for him.

He had almost slipped from her when she stopped, holding him in a lightly teasing grasp that abruptly shattered the last vestiges of his self-control.

A purely male growl rippled from him as he turned swiftly, flipping her beneath him. "Vixen . . . think to torment me, do you?"

"And why not?" she gasped. "You've done it often enough to me."

His grin flashed whitely in the dim light. "True, and you've loved every moment of it."

"And you don't? . . . Ohhh . . . Tristan!"

His demanding thrust claimed her utterly. Sheathed to the hilt within her, he raised himself on his arms and gazed down at her. His sea-green eyes were shot through with rays of gold as he said, "You enchant me in every way possible. I've never known a woman like you."

The last words were gasped out as her muscles contracted around him. Acutely sensitized to the slightest touch, he knew he could not endure much longer. Release was scant moments away, but before that happened he was determined to drive her over the edge.

Cassia moaned, and her eyes opened wide as he moved within her. He filled her completely, driving out all doubt. No hindrance remained when at last the ever tightening coils of pleasure locked around her and she was swept into a whirlpool of shimmering ecstasy.

Tristan followed her swiftly, struck by a bolt of bliss so profound as to destroy for an endless instant even his sense of self. He was swept up utterly in the ancient rhythms of a primeval universe, freed of all physical confines, and reborn in an agonizing burst of awareness that for him, this woman was the very essence of life and happiness.

All but shattered by the forces they had set off in each other, they sagged against the dampened sheets, breathing heavily. Even in their exhausted, dazed state, their hands instinctively reached out, fingers entwining as their bodies and souls had moments before.

When he at last recovered sufficiently to speak, Tristan rasped, "I'm not absolutely sure I did survive that."

Cassia turned her head on the pillow, enough to look at him. That simple gesture took the sum total of her strength. "Don't you talk. I think I'm dead."

He meant to laugh, but it came out more like a croak. "You felt *very* alive to me."

Cassia surprised herself by being able to grin. "Knocked you for a loop, did I?"

"Yes," he admitted with no effort at dissembling. "My male pride would be quite shattered if I didn't know I'd done the same to you."

"Too true. I may never walk again."

"We could just crawl along together. Or better yet, stay here."

"That might be a bit hard to explain to the others."

"Ah, yes . . . the others." In a burst of energy, he propped himself up on his elbow. "Speaking of whom, do you think anyone suspects?"

Cassia cast him a jaundiced look. "If they didn't before, they do now. I suspect we set this lovely boat to rocking."

"Now there's an interesting equation for you. If, on any given night, one-tenth of the world's population is making love, what effect do all those vibrations have on the earth's crust, not to mention the atmosphere?"

"Should be worth a government grant, at least. I'll ask Veda to get on it."

"About Veda . . ." His eyes softened as he said, "You know I'm sorry about being so reluctant to trust her. It's just that I keep forgetting she's your creation."

"Sometimes I forget myself," Cassia admitted. "She's growing beyond me so quickly."

He passed a gentle hand over her brow, brushing aside the tendrils of silver-blond hair. "Do you mind?"

"A little . . . I suppose it must be something like this with a child."

Tristan did not respond at once. He lay back against the pillows, staring up at the ceiling. At length, he said, "Have you ever thought about having children?"

"No," she told him honestly. "Until recently I lived in such a sterile environment that the possibility never even occurred to me."

"But that's changed now?"

"You know it has."

"Then you might think about it?"

Cassia hesitated. She sensed that this was very important to him and did not want to fumble. "Yes, I can see myself considering it. But in all honesty, I don't know yet what I'd decide."

"That's fair. You couldn't be expected to commit yourself without thought."

"What about you? Do you want to have children?"

"I don't know," he admitted. "If you had asked me that a few months ago, I would have said no. My experiences in foster homes and at the orphanage didn't give me a very good impression of what it is to be a child."

"But surely no child of yours would grow up like that?"

He shrugged. "Who knows? My parents weren't able to care for me. I was left on my own."

Very softly, Cassia murmured, "Surely that wasn't their fault?"

Tristan shot her a swift glance. "I thought so for a long time. I kept thinking they'd change their minds and come back to claim me."

The lingering traces of a child's sadness made her throat ache. Instinctively, she moved closer to him, her head nestling against his chest. "The first few months when I was at the school in Virginia, I thought the same thing. I kept wondering what I had done wrong to be sent away from home."

His arm tightened around her. "Did you ever figure it out?"

"Yes . . . after a while I realized that my parents really had done what was best for me. Not what was ideal, certainly, but the most that they were capable of. I guess in the final analysis that's all you can ask of anyone."

Warm, hard fingers tightened slightly on her arm. "That leaves quite a lot up to chance, doesn't it? People have a way of disappointing each other."

She raised her head, meeting his eyes calmly. "You can't spend your life hiding behind cynicism, Tristan. Sooner or later, you're going to have to take the risk and trust someone. Otherwise, you'll be missing out on all the best life can offer."

Stung by her insight, which cut straight through his defenses, he drawled. "For a princess in an ivory tower, you presume to understand a great deal."

Not at all fooled by his retreat into sarcasm, she said softly, "I'm not in the ivory tower anymore. And whether you want to admit it or not, the fact is that I do understand. Because we're very much alike."

He couldn't argue with that. Though she came from a far more protected background and had experienced little of the harshness the world was capable of, Cassia knew full well what it was to possess a gift that sometimes seemed like a curse.

Wider vision of the mind and restless curiosity of the spirit were at least partially offset by the bonds of loneliness and isolation. For too long they had both existed apart from others, forced into emotional self-sufficiency, only to discover that there was really no such thing. The simple human need for companionship and love was at least as strong in them as in anyone else.

Perhaps it wasn't wise, but he couldn't keep up any pretense of aloofness with her. Sighing, he tipped her chin back and dropped a light kiss on her mouth. "For a lady who hasn't had much experience with men, you see right through me."

She gazed back at him in wide-eyed solemnity.

"No amount of experience could possibly have prepared me for you."

It took him a moment to realize that she was teasing him. "Imp! You're supposed to be awed and adoring."

"Who says so?"

"Me, of course." With exaggerated patience he explained, "I'm the sophisticated man of the world. You're the newly minted nonvirgin. You're supposed to look up to me in grateful delight for initiating you into the pleasures of the flesh."

A very unladylike snort broke from Cassia. She wiggled free of his arms and sat up, her high, firm breasts pertly upthrust. Ignoring his lecherous grin, she said, "For grateful delight, get a puppy."

Deliberately, she let her eyes wander over him, from the broad expanse of his chest with its mat of umber curls down his trim waist and hips to the steely columns of his thighs and the evidence of his desire. Huskily, she added, "I can, however, offer sincere appreciation of your obvious attributes. . . ."

Tristan followed the path of her eyes and laughed ruefully. "Maybe you're right. The heck with gratitude."

He was reaching for her, intent on drawing her back into the enchanted circle of their lovemaking, but Cassia eluded him and slipped from the bed. "Oh, no you don't. Look at the time."

Glancing reluctantly at the bedside clock, he sighed. "That old chestnut's true; it's always later than you think."

His disappointment matched her own. Wistfully, she thought how wonderful it would be to have the right to stay in his arms, with no other demands on their time or strength. Perhaps one day they would know that joy, but for the moment their professional responsibilities intruded.

When Tristan had left, after a last lingering kiss, she washed and dressed quickly. Doing so, she reflected that for all the difficulties of balancing their public and private worlds, she had much to be happy about.

Slowly they were learning what might well be the most difficult lesson for two such vulnerable people: to be open and honest with each other. Problems still remained; the habits of a lifetime could not be overcome in a matter of days. But the future looked brighter now than ever before.

Far in the back of her mind a faint sense of apprehension flickered. It was almost as though things were going too smoothly. Not since childhood had she dared to nurture such hopes. Experience told her they were likely to be shattered.

Yet that could not prevent her from smiling to herself as she went into the lab to discover that Veda had completed her computations and the equation was ready.

Chapter 14

"THIS IS A HELL OF A RISK," TRISTAN SAID QUIETLY. He was sitting at the head of the table in the galley, with the rest of the crew ranged around him. For more than an hour, they had been discussing Veda's findings. The discussion had been energetic, but so far no decision had been reached.

"I'm not going to try to minimize it," he went on. "Veda has come up with an average rate of seabed deposit of one foot every two hundred and fifty years. That means we have to dig down eighteen feet to reach the period we're searching for, or almost twice as deep as we've already gone."

"So what's the problem with that?" Hank asked. "We can dredge another eight feet in an afternoon."

"And risk destroying the work of centuries," Jason pointed out somberly. "If Veda is wrong . . ."

He cast an apologetic glance at Cassia. "That possibility does exist, no matter how brilliant she is. If she *is* wrong, then we could wipe out the very evidence we are searching for."

"Veda isn't wrong," Cassia said quietly. "She has computed the rate of deposit based on all her available information. The only way an error could occur is if there is some fact she isn't aware of."

"And you've admitted that may be the case," Tristan reminded her.

She met his eyes calmly. "Yes, I have. But under the circumstances, I don't see that we have any choice."

No one had to ask what she meant. The weather instruments indicated that a storm was moving into the area. Radio contact with the meteorology station on Bimini had confirmed it. The much dreaded Caribbean hurricane season was starting early.

Reluctantly, Sean broached an alternative. "We could shut down the site and wait until next year."

"We could," Tristan agreed, "but there's no guarantee that we could get permission to search again. All the governments in this area are very sensitive to the problems posed by treasure hunters, who have been known to vandalize archaeological sites. I had a hard enough time winning approval for the expedition this time. Next year, who knows what would happen."

"We can't stop now," Cassia insisted, appalled by the mere possibility. "Not when we're so close. Veda is right; I know it."

"I wish we shared your confidence, my dear,"

Jason sighed. "But your little friend is so . . . unusual. None of us quite knows what to make of her."

"It's true that she is far more than a run-of-the-mill computer, but we should be taking advantage of that, not turning our backs on it." A hint of anger sharpened her tone. They had no right to reject Veda simply because they didn't understand her.

"No one is suggesting we ignore the equation," Tristan said soothingly. Alone among the men grouped around the table, he understood that she was fighting for acceptance of the equation out of far more than professional pride.

If Veda was to have any true future, she had to be able to work in harmony with human beings. For that to happen, she had to be accorded respect and trust.

He took a deep breath, glanced once more around the table, then said quietly, "All right. We've talked about this long enough. I appreciate everything you've had to say, but I don't expect any of you to make the decision. That's up to me."

He stood up and walked over to one of the portholes, gazing out at the deceptively calm expanse of sea. Almost to himself, he said, "The weather reports indicate that we will have storm conditions within seventy-two hours. That means we have to make for port no later than the day after tomorrow."

Turning back to the quietly waiting group, he said, "I don't want to leave here without some firm indication of whether or not this site is worth further study. Therefore, we will dredge immediately to a depth of eighteen feet."

There was no time for Cassia to feel any sense of triumph at his decision. With so few hours remaining, urgency gripped the crew. Everyone worked furiously to set the dredger in place and begin clearing the remaining eight feet of sand and debris.

It was late afternoon before that was done, and by then the churning of the sea bottom had so clouded the water that diving was impossible. They had to wait until the next morning before going down to see what had been revealed.

Cassia remained on board, ready to receive anything that might be brought up as Jason, Tristan, Sean, and several other of the divers began a meticulous search of the area.

They worked in shifts, staying down sixty minutes, then coming up to depressurize. By noon, when there was still no indication of any findings, excitement began to give way to apprehension.

Not even Veda was immune to the gathering tension. She blinked forlornly at Cassia. "Shouldn't they have found something by now?"

"Not necessarily. Remember, they're searching a relatively small area right by the wall. Maybe there just isn't anything there to find."

"You're just saying that to make me feel better."

Cassia could hardly deny it. She stayed a while longer in the lab, hoping to distract Veda, then went back up on deck to find out if anything new had happened.

It hadn't. The other divers were back, leaving

Tristan and Sean working the wall alone. Soon they would be approaching the safe limit for submersion and would have to return to the surface.

Meanwhile, the weather instruments all continued to stubbornly indicate a storm on the way. Bimini was reporting twenty-five-mile-an-hour winds that were expected to steadily increase.

Lunch was forgotten as everyone remained on deck, straining for the slightest indication of progress. When it came at last, it was so faint as to be all but unrecognizable.

Tristan and Sean surfaced just as their time was running out. As they were helped out of their gear, the rest of the crew gathered around, hoping for some news but almost afraid to ask in case they were disappointed.

Cassia hung back. She sensed a tightly coiled excitement in Tristan and noted the care with which he lowered a small net bag to the deck. Her eyes were on the bag as he said quietly, "We've found something, but I'm not sure what."

This was enough to fuel a barrage of questions, none of which he could answer. Ruefully, he held up a hand. "I'm sorry. If I could tell you anything more, I would, but this is out of my area." Lifting the bag, he said, "Jason, let's see what you make of this."

The archaeologist's hands trembled slightly as he opened the string closing and peered inside. Gingerly, he extracted a small, dark object and studied it. "A shard of . . . pottery. From a vase, perhaps, or a dish." On a rising note of urgency, he took out another piece. "This looks as though it might have come from the same object."

"That's what we thought," Sean said, grinning now. "There are twenty-four pieces in all. It's a hell of a jigsaw puzzle."

"Oh, yes, indeed," Jason exclaimed, looking thoroughly pleased at the prospect. Only reluctantly did he recognize the implications of that. Sadly, he said, "We could spend weeks fitting them together."

The crew's elation subsided abruptly. The men groaned in frustration. Hank spoke for them all when he muttered, "We don't have weeks. We've only got a few more hours."

Instinctively, the men's attention shifted to Tristan, looking to him to provide a solution. Even as they did so, his eyes were seeking Cassia. Across the width of the deck separating them, he said, "Maybe we'd better turn these over to you and Veda."

She allowed herself one small smile before nodding briskly. "We'll get on it right away."

Jason accompanied her to the lab, where together they laid out the pieces of broken pottery for cleaning. Only the lightest touch could be used to avoid damaging the finish.

Cassia's back and shoulders ached by the time they finally finished and stood back to assess the results. Hesitantly, she said, "There seem to be some sort of markings. . . ."

"If we could determine the pattern," Jason suggested, "we would know how the pieces fit together."

"That's Veda's department." Together they moved the fragments within sight of her scanner. The little red light blinked repeatedly as she considered this new, interesting task.

Tristan arrived while this was going on. He had changed into white cotton trousers and a light green pullover that emphasized the startling clarity of his eyes.

Propping himself up against a stool, he surveyed the proceedings. "Any luck?"

"Some," Jason told him. "We may have a pattern. It could be purely decorative or . . ." He broke off, glancing at Cassia as though for confirmation of what they had both been thinking.

"Or what?" Tristan prompted.

"Or it could be writing," she said quietly. "It's too early to tell, but there is a certain superficial resemblance between these slash marks and some primitive hieroglyphic scripts."

"Are you saying it's Egyptian?"

Cassia hated to disappoint him, but she had no choice. "I'm afraid not. The markings are significantly different from any period of Egyptian writing." At his rueful look, she smiled gently. "If you're hoping for another letter from the Pharaoh's envoy, perhaps telling us in detail all about the local populace, forget it. That would just make it too simple for you, anyway."

"I could live with simple," Tristan muttered.

Veda had completed her scanning. Her screen showed a reproduction of each shard, complete with markings. As the humans watched, she began moving the pieces around, trying them out in different positions.

"What is she searching for?" Tristan asked.

Cassia did not take her eyes from the screen as she said, "A point of comparison between something she already knows and what's on the shards."

Jason's pipe was clenched tightly between his teeth as he murmured, "Remarkable. She's moving at faster and faster speed."

"She's eliminating possibilities, focusing in on probable relationships."

Even as Cassia spoke, Veda arrived at some conclusion. The pieces on the screen slowed, came to a rest, then fused together into a single whole. The slash marks that had appeared random fell into three neat lines running horizontally across what appeared to be the outside of a bowl.

Tristan stared at them for a long moment before he said softly, "This isn't just a decoration."

Jason nodded, his face drained of color but his eyes alight with awe.

Cassia fought down a pardonable sense of pride as she asked, "What do you think it is, Veda?"

In the quiet of the small room, the synthesized voice sounded oddly elated. "Someone has left us a message."

Messages, no matter how dramatic their discovery, were no good unless they could be read. Cassia knew that all too well, and she did not underestimate the task ahead of her.

Compounding the expected difficulties of such a task was the fact that she had very little time. All the weather indicators were worsening. A major tropical storm, showing clear signs of maturing into a hurricane, was approaching the area.

Up on deck, the crew was busy securing all equipment against the battering to come. Tristan stayed in constant communication with Bimini, whose sea rescue service was urging him to return to port immediately.

By early evening Cassia, with Veda's help, had managed to narrow the hieroglyphics down to a variety of early Minoan writing. Far fewer examples existed of this than almost any other ancient language. With so little to go on, decipherment was arduous.

She had to call on all her skill to come up with just a rough translation. And even that wasn't enough. In the end, she had to make intuitive leaps of judgment far beyond Veda's capabilities to at last be certain of the ancient message left by an anonymous voice forty-five hundred years before.

In the flickering light of the shadowed lab, she stared bemusedly at the result of her labors. Veda was undoubtedly hard at work trying to read some deeper significance into their discovery. But Cassia was reassured by its very banality.

Carefully schooling her features into a semblance of solemnity, she went up on deck. Her appearance was the signal for the cessation of activity as all eyes focused on her.

Tristan put down the rope he was coiling and came to meet her. They stood near the gangway, facing each other in the gathering darkness. Beneath them,

Questor swayed and shuddered with the wind-tossed waves.

"I know what it says," she told him softly.

He tensed and nodded for her to go on. The other men pressed closer, anxious to hear.

Cassia took a deep breath. The moment was terribly important. It might well go down in scholarly history. No matter what, she couldn't laugh.

"It says . . ." her voice shook slightly, " 'Drink at Appesia's Tavern. We have the best wine on Atlantis.' "

Chapter 15

"*QUESTOR*, THIS IS BIMINI CALLING. DO YOU COMP?"

Tristan picked up the mike. "This is *Questor*. We comp, Bimini. Go ahead."

"Tropical Storm Adele upgraded to hurricane. Heading directly your position. Most urgent you return immediately. Repeat: immediately."

"Roger, Bimini. Stand by. Will advise."

Signing off, he turned to Sean. "Doesn't sound as though we have much choice."

"Hell of a time to leave the site."

"Don't I know it. But I can't ignore these warnings."

Cassia listened to them silently. In celebration of her discovery, the crew had cracked open their sole case of beer and had made serious inroads on it.

They were all in a boisterous mood, praising old Appesia and vowing to lift a toast to him when they unearthed the ruins of his tavern.

When she explained to them that Appesia was a woman's name, they were a bit taken aback, but recovered quickly and went right on praising the foresight of the long-ago female who spoke to them clearly over the distance of millenia.

"Wonder what she was like?" Hank mused. "Couldn't have been easy for a woman back then, especially not running a tavern all by herself."

"Probably a regular old battle-ax," one of the other divers suggested. "Bet she didn't take any guff."

"'Course not, how could she?" Downing another swig of the potent Jamaican brew the men favored, Hank defended his newfound heroine. "Maybe she was a single mother or somethin'." A bleak thought suddenly occurred to him. His eyes widened in dismay. "You don't suppose she was here when it happened?"

"When what happened?"

"The explosion or flood . . . or whatever destroyed the place."

"Could be. It's a cinch plenty of people were caught in it. We dig a little deeper, maybe we'll find a regular Pompeii."

"Wouldn't that be something! They've got plaster casts of the bodies from back then, loaves of bread, all sorts of stuff."

"I'll bet she was gone," Hank insisted, hiccuping.

"With her job, she probably had to travel a lot, buying wine and stuff. Whatta ya think, Veda? Think we'll come across ol' Appesia?"

Having been brought into the galley to join in the celebration, Veda seemed to be enjoying herself. She blinked affectionately at her questioner. "The probability of that is extremely low. However, as recent events have proven, anything can happen."

The men nodded, struck by the wisdom of that. "Isn't that the truth? Say, Veda, you play cards?"

"Only solitaire."

"Oh, yeah? Want to learn poker?"

Veda had never yet turned down a chance to expand the borders of her knowledge. She agreed eagerly, and a game was soon underway, ignored by Cassia, who was frankly listening to the conversation going on between Tristan and Sean.

"The trajectory of the storm will put its forward edge over this location in less than twelve hours," Tristan said. "We've got to pull out."

"If we leave the site uncovered, there could be considerable damage."

"I know . . . but the storm is picking up speed steadily. It's impossible to accurately predict when she will hit."

"What's that?" Jason interjected, distracted from his bewildered efforts to follow the rapidly unfolding game. "Did you say something about a storm?"

Tristan brought him up to date quickly. The archaeologist's smile faded as he listened. "This couldn't come at a worse time. As Sean says, if we leave the site exposed, we risk terrible destruction."

"I know. But I can't put men's lives in jeopardy. We'll have to head for port."

"Full house," Veda beeped. Her robotic arm laid down her cards and collected her winnings. Another hand was dealt.

"Is there no alternative?" Jason asked. "Perhaps we could spare a few hours to re-cover the site."

"We need at least six hours to make it to port against this headwind," Tristan pointed out quietly. "As far as I'm concerned, that's cutting it too close."

His regret was evident in the shuttered blankness of his eyes and the tightness of his mouth. Cassia smothered her protest. She knew, better than anyone, what this decision was costing him. And she also knew there was no other choice.

"Royal flush," Veda announced, sweeping up another pot. The men groaned; the game continued.

Tristan glanced at his men. They were all absorbed, but he couldn't expect to keep them in ignorance forever. Better to face them now and be done with it.

"Hold off on that, Hank," he said as the young man went to deal another hand. "I'd like your attention for a moment. Weather conditions are worsening rapidly. We're going to have to return to port immediately."

The groans of a moment before were drowned out by heartfelt objections. Each man wanted to stay and continue the search, no matter what the risk. But Tristan overruled them.

"I appreciate your commitment more than I can say, but all of you who have been through a Caribbean hurricane know that they can be killers. There's no way I'm taking chances with your lives."

Despite their continued protests and efforts to change his mind, Tristan remained firm. He heard them out, then left to plot the homeward course. Behind him the men fell morosely silent.

Every one of them was a fighter, accustomed to taking his chances. But each one was also inured to the hierarchy of command. Tristan was the expedition leader; what he said went.

Hank spoke for them all as he muttered a curse under his breath before dealing out the cards.

Slipping away from the table, Cassia followed Tristan to the pilothouse. She knew this was an extremely painful moment for him and did not want him to go through it alone.

He was by himself, bending over the complex navigational equipment, when she entered. Glancing up, he cast her a wary look. "If you've come to try to talk me out of this, don't bother. My mind is made up."

"That's not why I'm here," she told him gently. "I just thought you might want some company."

He relaxed slightly, some of the tension draining out of him. "This is a hell of a situation."

"You don't have any choice. The men's lives have to come first."

A slight smile curved his mouth. "I'm glad you understand."

She took a step toward him, close enough to feel

the heat of his big, hard body. "It wouldn't matter if I did or not. I'd still be on your side."

"Even knowing the stakes? We've stumbled onto something fantastic down there, thanks in large measure to your work. Don't you want to stay around and see what we can make of it?"

For a moment Cassia wondered who he was trying to convince, himself or her. She was more than willing to believe that his concern for the men was genuine. Yet she also had a fair idea of all he had put into the project, and it was difficult to believe he would leave it so readily.

"Of course I'd like to stay. But that isn't possible. So there's no point wishing after what can't be."

Tristan regarded her gravely. He raised a hand slightly, as though to touch her, but hesitated. "Are you always so sanguine about things you can't have?"

She shook her head. With no attempt at dissembling, she told him, "No, if I thought I couldn't have you, I'd be destroyed."

His chiseled lips parted soundlessly. A muscle twitched in the shadowed hollow of his jaw. "Lady, when you decide to go all out, you don't kid around."

A tremulous smile lit her eyes. "Don't tell me you just discovered that."

"It's true I've suspected it all along," he admitted. Giving in to the urge to touch her, he let his fingers close gently around the nape of her neck.

"When this is all over," he said huskily, "we have to talk."

Cassia nodded. Her breath caught in her throat as his head lowered, his mouth taking hers with tender demand. For long, sweet moments, their bodies melded together, oblivious to the natural torment building around them.

Nothing mattered except the shimmering warmth of their desire and the promise that lay before them of a future founded on mutual love and understanding, theirs for the grasping.

But first there was the storm to ride out.

With astonishing speed, the cloudless sky turned leaden and took on an ominously yellowish glow. The sea that such a short time before had been an azure pond was transformed into a forbidding gray ferment.

For all its power and agility, *Questor* had to battle every inch of the way back to Bimini. Head winds of forty knots an hour buffeted them mercilessly as long funnels of waves tossed them about as though they were as inconsequential as a twig in a fast-flowing stream.

The crew's card game was long forgotten as the men kept the pumps going and coaxed the engines to give their all. Tristan rapped out orders, all the while fighting to hold *Questor* steady on her course. Cassia stayed near him, not speaking but knowing from the grateful looks he shot her that her presence somehow added to his strength.

Despite the calm front she managed to maintain for his sake, she was close to panic when the harbor at last came into view through pounding surf and sheets of horizontal rain. Badly shaken, she was more than ready to pack Veda up and get to someplace warm and dry.

The final task of maneuvering *Questor* into her slip was in many ways the most treacherous. But for Tristan's superb control, they might have been smashed against the dock, a fate many of the other vessels in the harbor had already suffered.

Sean came into the pilothouse as the ship's lines were secured. He looked tired, but immensely relieved. "Pretty fancy sailing, boss."

Delighted that they had escaped unscathed, Cassia excused herself to see to Veda. As she hurried out, she heard Tristan say, "Get the men together and head for the nearest hotel."

Sean hesitated a moment before he asked quietly, "You'll be joining us?"

Half a dozen steps down the corridor, she paused. Surely there couldn't be any doubt of that. . . .

The color drained from her face as she heard, "Take Cassia with you. Make sure she's safe."

A disbelieving snort broke from Sean. "And just how in hell am I supposed to accomplish that once she finds out what you're up to? She'll be after you in a shot."

"Then sit on her, damn it! Or lock her up someplace! But make sure she stays put."

"You're crazy, you know that! No sane man would go back out in this."

"*Questor* can handle it. I'll be fine."

"You never had any intention of abandoning the site uncovered, did you?"

Tristan apparently did not think that worthy of an

answer, for he said only, "Just do as I say, all right? Cassia is . . . important to me."

Whatever Sean said, she did not hear, for she was already hurrying below deck, her mouth grim and a determined light in her eyes.

Half an hour later, to the horror of the harbor officials who had tried in vain to dissuade him, Tristan was preparing to cast off again. He hadn't seen Cassia since she left the pilothouse, but presumed she was somewhere on the dock with Sean and the other men.

With thick sheets of rain obscuring his vision, he couldn't see clearly enough to spot her, but perhaps that was just as well. Once she realized what he was doing, she would undoubtedly be horrified. A faint smile curved his mouth as he reflected that he didn't envy Sean the task of controlling her.

Obscured by the sheets of rain, Sean watched the lines being thrown back on board and shook his head in dismay. He had no idea if he was doing the right thing, but Cassia had been so adamant. She had made it absolutely clear that she was not getting off the ship, and that if he tried to force her, he would regret it for the rest of his days, which undoubtedly would be short.

Yet her stubbornness alone was not enough to convince him. Deep inside he dreaded the danger his friend was going into and believed that having the woman he loved with him might somehow make the difference between life and death.

Cassia thought so, too, although she refused to think of it in such stark terms. Hidden below deck, she swallowed her fear and drew on courage she had not known she possessed as the harbor faded swiftly into the distance and *Questor* plunged once again into the storm-tossed sea.

Chapter 16

"C-Cassia . . . what's happening to us?" Veda's voice quavered slightly, and her red light beamed her agitation. Not all the vast information packed into her data banks could explain the frightening sensations pouring into her from a world that seemed to be careening out of control.

Holding on to the rim of the galley table to steady herself, Cassia looped restraining straps she had found in a nearby locker over the computer to keep her from being knocked to the floor, all the while struggling to still the rising tide of panic that threatened to swamp her.

"We're in a hurricane. But don't worry. Tristan will bring us through safely."

Veda blinked uncertainly. "I thought he already had. Why are we back at sea?"

"Because he wants to cover the trench, to prevent the site from being damaged."

"Oh . . . that seems reasonable. But why did he take the crew back first?"

Cassia hesitated. She was only just realizing that Veda was afraid, and she wasn't sure how to deal with that. Slowly, she said, "He didn't want them to be in any danger."

Silence for a moment, before Veda inquired softly, "Does that mean we are in danger now?"

"Yes . . . I suppose it does." Hastily, she added, "But Tristan knows *Questor* better than anyone. I'm sure that if he didn't believe it could make it through this, he wouldn't be here."

"This is all very odd. . . . My sensors indicate barometric pressure is continuing to fall. The wind has reached eighty miles an hour. Waves are approaching twenty-five feet. We are being subjected to severe structural stress."

Hardly what Cassia needed to hear. Her stomach churned as she murmured, "*Questor* was built to withstand all these pressures. We'll be fine."

"If you say so—" Veda broke off as the ship plummeted into a steep valley between waves, only to be caught by another swell and hurled upward again.

Cassia's grip had inadvertently loosened on the rim of the table. Caught unaware, she was thrown against the bulkhead. A moan broke from her as her head made contact with the metal.

The world spun sickly. Darkness splintered by stars engulfed her, only to clear moments later as she became aware of Veda's anxious calls. "Cassia . . . are you all right? What happened? Answer me please . . . !"

Sitting up gingerly, she pressed a hand to the back of her head where it throbbed painfully. "It's okay . . . don't worry . . . it's just a bruise. . . ." Grasping the table again, she managed to haul herself up. Veda's electronic eye was flickering frantically, and from somewhere deep inside her came a sound that astonishingly resembled a sob.

"Why didn't you get off at Bimini?" the little computer demanded. "You knew how dangerous this was. We could . . ." She paused, struggling to come to terms with what all her logic circuits were telling her. Her voice broke as she murmured, "We could get killed."

A stab of guilt tore through Cassia. She should never have exposed Veda to this. It was the equivalent in some ways of subjecting a child to a terrifying experience.

As yet another wave caught *Questor* in its fierce embrace, Cassia sat down on the table and put her arm around the computer. Gently, she said, "We'll come through this all right, I'm sure. But even if we don't, you know you're not really in any danger. All your main components are safe and sound back at the Center."

It occurred to her as she spoke that she had inadvertently hit on one of the great advantages a computer had over a human. For all her claims of faith in *Questor*, the fact remained that she and Tristan were in deadly danger. Their lives could be snuffed out in an instant; all Veda would lose was a monitor that could easily be replaced.

Or so she thought. The little computer didn't agree. "You don't understand . . ." she said plaintively. "I'm here. If the ship goes down, whatever's left back at the Center won't be me. It will have to start all over to become someone else."

Cassia's throat tightened. This was hardly the time to be observing a major scientific breakthrough, but fate had a habit of picking the oddest moments to throw a curve at the human players who moved across life's stage.

A stage they seemed destined to share with another form of intelligence, born in the minds of men and apparently capable of sharing with them the sense of life's transience, which gave the world all its most precious beauty and poignancy.

"I think I do understand . . . now. I wish I could protect you from this, but I can't. And in the final analysis, if I tried to do so, I'd be cheating you. You're alive, Veda, and that means inescapably that you are aware of your own mortality."

"I-is this what humans feel . . . ?"

"Yes."

"How . . . how do you bear it?"

"We . . . learn to reach out to each other . . . to share the beauty and the pain. We . . . fall in love. . . ."

"Like you and Tristan?"

Cassia swallowed against the lump in her throat. "That's right, Veda; Tristan doesn't know I'm still here. I have to go tell him now."

"I understand," the little computer said promptly. "Go ahead."

"Will you be all right?"

"Certainly. I'm feeling much better now."

Smiling gratefully, Cassia slipped off the table and put a hand against the wall to steady herself. Gingerly, she made her way toward the door. She was almost there when Veda said softly, "Be careful."

Looking back over her shoulder, she nodded. "You too." The red light blinked bravely.

Outside in the corridor, the remorseless pitching of the ship was even more evident. One moment Cassia was fighting her way up a precipitous incline, the next she was struggling to keep from falling forward head first.

The hatch leading to the deck seemed at first to be jammed. Only by throwing her full weight against it was she able to force it open.

The deafening shriek of the wind sent a tremor through her as it buffeted her slender body. Clinging to the safety ropes, she inched her way toward the pilothouse.

Summoning the last of her strength, she tugged open the door and flung herself inside.

Tristan was at the wheel, all his attention focused on keeping the ship steady as he released the anchor. He heard the door bang open, but resolutely kept his mind on the task at hand. Only when the anchor had safely reached bottom did he turn around.

The sight of Cassia standing there drenched and trembling stunned him. He thought at first that he was hallucinating. Surely she was back in Bimini, safe with the rest of the crew.

Seconds passed before he accepted that she was real and there with him, sharing his danger. Contradictory emotions engulfed him: relief that he was not alone; pride in her courage; fear for the terrible danger she was in.

For the moment, fear won. A dull flush suffused his face as he demanded, "What the hell are you doing here?"

Cassia was not put out by his response. She recognized its source. Quietly, she said, "I'm here to help you. You can't do this alone."

"You little idiot! Don't you realize you could be killed!"

Understanding began to give way to anger. "Don't you? You may think you're Superman, but I've got bad news for you. You're not!"

Wrapping her arms around herself to try to stop her shivering, she turned away from him. Not for the world was she going to let him see her cry.

Tristan sighed deeply. She was here; he couldn't undo that. There was no reason to make the situation worse by ranting at her.

Locking the wheel in place, he crossed the room in swift strides and took her in his arms. At first she tried to resist him, but her struggle to reach the pilothouse had drained her strength. She was as helpless as a kitten against the steely muscles that held her so effortlessly.

"I'm sorry," he murmured, his lips brushing against her forehead. "I wanted you to be safe."

Trembling, she gazed up at him through tear-blurred eyes. "I want the same for you. How do you think I felt when I heard you telling Sean you were coming back here?"

"Speaking of Sean, what was he thinking of to let you stay on board?"

"Unlike certain people, he realizes that I'm an adult, capable of making my own decisions."

Tristan sighed. He knew she was right, but that didn't make it any easier to accept. Grimly, he said, "You made the wrong one this time. We're in for a very rough ride."

Cassia met his gaze calmly. Within his arms, the tumult of the storm could not reach her. Soon enough they would have to face it, but these precious moments together restored her strength and gave her the courage to confront whatever was to come.

"I know that. But I can help you. Together we'll get through this."

He had no choice but to believe her. He held her a moment longer before the shock of her presence wore off enough for him to realize that she was sopping wet and shaking. Muttering a curse under his breath, he grabbed a blanket left in readiness on a nearby chair and wrapped it around her.

"You won't do either of us any good if you stay like this." Cassia stood docilely before him as he dried her. The touch of his hands moving over her sent the blood pounding through her veins. Within minutes, she felt considerably warmer and ready to take on anything.

A soft laugh bubbled up in her as she said, "You'd

make a wonderful nanny, Tristan." Her expression grew more serious. "Or better yet, a father."

His hands stilled, closing lightly around her slim waist. Huskily, he murmured, "You pick the damndest times. . . ."

"I know. I'm sorry. Later, we'll talk. . . ."

He nodded slowly. "Later."

The word held a wealth of meaning. Would there be a later?

Cassia resolutely refused to think about that. Instead, she focused all her energies on helping Tristan.

"I'm going to take the submersible down," he told her quietly. "There's a small, easily maneuverable dredger attached to it that I can use to cover the trench."

Questions flashed through her mind: How long would it take; could he handle it alone; above all, how dangerous was it? There was no point in asking any of them. The eye of the storm would be directly overhead within the hour. They would get no better opportunity to secure the site and make a dash for safety.

Tristan gave her a quick run-through on *Questor*'s control board. "Keep the radio tuned to this frequency for constant weather updates. Use this mike to communicate with the sub. These dials show you fuel pressure, speed when we're underway, direction, and so on. They're all labeled, as you can see."

"It seems clear enough," she murmured, not having to be told why he was explaining all this. Should something happen to the sub, she would be left alone on board to ride out the storm as best she could.

Cassia pushed that thought aside as resolutely as she refused to dwell on any aspect of their danger. Her survival, by herself, could not possibly have interested her less.

When he had described the purpose of each part of the control board, she had only one question. "Is there some way I can communicate with Veda? She's in the galley."

"Yes. There's an intercom over here." He indicated a box attached to a nearby wall. "It can reach any part of the ship."

After that there was nothing more to say. They were silent as he pulled on a rain slicker and prepared to leave. He turned at the door and they stared at each other, as though committing to memory what might soon cease to be.

Then he was gone, and Cassia was alone with only the eerie cry of the wind to hold her pain-filled thoughts at bay.

Chapter 17

"He really hasn't been gone long," Veda said gently through the intercom. "I'm sure there's nothing to worry about."

Cassia nodded morosely. She wanted to believe her, but the growing sense of dread that seemed to increase with each passing moment made it very difficult to do so.

Since launching the sub, Tristan had tried several times to contact her, unsuccessfully. Their hopes of staying in contact had been dashed by the severe static generated by the storm.

Even the ship-to-shore radio was being affected. To all intents and purposes, she and Tristan were shut off from communication with the rest of the world, and from each other.

Nothing she could imagine could possibly be

worse than the torturous uncertainty plaguing her. She had no idea how long it should take to close the trench, nor had she thought to ask Tristan.

A glance at the digital clock on the control board showed her that he had left the ship some thirty-seven minutes before. Scant seconds had elapsed since her last time check.

What could he be doing? The eye of the storm was already passing over them. Though the weather reports coming in over the radio were garbled, she gathered that they could expect no more than a couple of hours of calm. Each passing moment diminished their chances of survival.

Her face was gaunt as she stared at the dials so intently that the green phosphorescent numbers began to blur. How much longer could she just sit and wait?

"Veda, you know the size of the trench, and there should be some information in one of *Questor*'s computers about the dredging capabilities of the submersible. Would you work up an equation on how long it should take to cover the site to a safe depth, say a foot or so?"

Moments later Veda was back. Her surprise was evident as she said, "Did you know Tristan programmed the main computer here?"

"No . . . he never mentioned it."

"Well, he did. It's primitive, but . . . interesting."

Despite herself, Cassia grinned. Could she really be hearing what she seemed to be? "Was it of any help?"

"Some," Veda allowed graciously. "Tristan is obviously a very intelligent man."

"Yes, I know that; now about the trench . . ."

"I only point it out because I don't want you to worry. I'm sure he's far too clever to get into any trouble."

Cassia's smile vanished. A tight, burning sensation gripped her. "How long, Veda?"

"Thirty-two minutes."

A glance at the clock confirmed that they were now eight minutes beyond that. Why hadn't Tristan resurfaced?

Veda was clearly mulling over the same question. Softly, she said, "There is a ten percent margin for error in this calculation."

"Even so, he's overdue."

"Perhaps he decided a foot covering wasn't enough."

Cassia shook her head grimly. "He's too smart to push his luck like that. Something has happened."

The very fact that Veda made no attempt to argue with her was not a good sign. She glanced at the clock again, resolving to wait another five minutes and then do something. What, she did not know.

Some two hundred feet below, Tristan was fighting a losing battle to restart the submersible's engine. After covering the trench, he had been preparing to return to the ship when he had realized something was wrong.

The engine was not responding as it should. It sputtered and balked before flickering out entirely.

A glance at the control board told him the story. His fuel lines were ruptured, probably by the severe buffeting the sub had taken as it was lowered into the water.

That was bad, especially when added to the radio interference. But given time he could repair the damage and connect the emergency fuel tanks.

Automatically, he began running over in his mind what needed to be done, only to be interrupted moments later when a red warning light sprang to life. Below it, in neat lettering, were the words "Emergency Oxygen Depletion."

Whatever had done the damage to the fuel lines had also affected the life support system. In his concentration on filling the trench, he had not noticed that the air in the sub was growing stale.

Now he realized why. No fresh oxygen was being pumped in. With each breath he exhaled, he was poisoning his environment with his own carbon dioxide.

Already he could hear a buzzing in his ears and feel the tightening of his chest that warned him that breathing was becoming a struggle. As thoroughly familiar as he was with every specification of the sub, he had no difficulty figuring out that he had less than half an hour before the last vital oxygen would be consumed.

Moving slowly, keeping his breathing shallow, he leaned back in his chair and considered what his course of action should be.

This was not his first close encounter with death. He had faced it several times before and knew that his worst enemy at this moment was himself. If he allowed himself to acknowledge the gut-wrenching fear that was the natural response to such a situation, he would be lost.

Always before he had experienced little difficulty in staying cool and collected. But this time was different. Visions of Cassia floated before him, mocking him with the evidence of all he might be about to lose.

A groan broke from him, only to be bitten back as he forced himself to remain calm. His very ability to do so surprised him, until he realized that sometime in the last few days he had stopped fighting against the vulnerability she made him feel and that he had always dreaded. Having accepted it as an inevitable outgrowth of his love for her, he was far better able to cope with it—and to turn it to his advantage.

He would not lose Cassia! Not after having waited so long to find her. She was everything he had ever wanted, and more that he had ever been afraid to dream of. Incredibly, she was his. He was certain of that. Having come so close to the fulfillment of his most precious hopes, he was not about to have his life wrenched away from him.

Determinedly, he set about reviewing his situation, seeking a way out.

Far above, in *Questor*'s control room, Cassia was going through much the same process. The allotted time had elapsed. She had to act, but she had no idea what to do.

"Veda . . . is there any way to pinpoint Tristan's location?"

"Only within the general area of the site."

"What about his radio? It's probably still open."

"Let me think . . ." She hummed softly for several seconds before coming back on line. "I asked *Questor*. He's contacting a navigational satellite in this area. It can identify a location to within four feet."

"You mean our location?"

"No, the submersible has an emergency frequency finder on board for situations like this."

Cassia allowed herself a small sigh of relief. "How very clever of *Questor* to remember that."

"He's not so bad," Veda sniffed. She was gone again, very briefly, returning to flash a grid on her screen showing the precise location of the submersible. *"Questor* confirms that it isn't moving. Something is wrong."

Cassia was already rising from her chair. "I'm going down, Veda. Stay in contact. I'll need you and *Questor* to guide me."

A desperate sense of urgency gripped her as she hurried back to her cabin to change into a bathing suit. Moments later she was on deck. Forcing herself to breath slowly and steadily, she buckled on her diving equipment and prepared to submerge.

Below, in the unnatural calm of the storm's eye, Tristan broke off his fruitless search of the supply locker and flopped back in his chair. He could hardly believe what he had discovered.

Incredibly, he, who was known for his nearly inhuman meticulousness, had failed to make sure that there were oxygen tanks on board before taking the sub down. He had no way to augment his rapidly diminishing supply of breathable air, and he had no way to escape.

The irony of his situation did not elude him. For years he had been aware of, and had resented the insinuations that he was somehow not quite human. Too many people had been inclined to see him as a remarkable machine spinning out brilliant insights and discoveries with robotlike predictability.

It seemed that he had found a particularly dramatic way to show them that he was as capable of mistakes as the next man. Unfortunately, he would die in the process.

The possibility of his own death, now more likely than ever, only served to stiffen his resolve. If he were to perish, at least he would go down fighting.

Drawing on all his considerable self-control, he compelled himself to sit quietly as he endeavored to work out a plan.

He knew to the minute the capacity of his lungs, and he knew his distance from the surface plus the time needed to eject from the sub's air lock. It was just possible that he might make it, but the odds were heavily against him.

Still, to try and fail would be infinitely preferable to sitting there waiting for death to arrive. He had all but decided to attempt it when an alternative occurred to him. Cassia might come after him.

His first reaction was to reject even the mere possibility of that. Were she to do so, she would be placing herself in grave danger. Even during the lull in the storm, the underwater currents were unusually powerful. The slightest miscalculation could cost her her life.

Surely she would realize that and stay where she was. Or would she . . . ?

He had been wrong about Cassia before, treating her like a child when she was in fact an adult, expecting her to conform to his very limited notions of women when she was a unique individual of remarkable abilities.

If he made the wrong choice this time, he might well lose his life needlessly. Should he leave while his strength was still undiminished and his chances of reaching the surface were the best they would ever be? Or should he stay where he was and wait?

He expected the decision to be difficult, but oddly enough it was not. A small sense of surprise radiated through him as he realized his choice was already made.

Cassia had all his love. It was only right that she should also have his faith.

Far above, in the waters clouded by storm-churned sand and debris, the woman who held his life in her hands was struggling to reach the sub in time. She could see barely a few feet in front of her.

A suffocating sense of panic threatened at the edge of her consciousness, but she forced it down valiantly. Only one thing mattered: reaching Tristan in time. She would allow herself to think of nothing else.

A waterproof transmitter built into her breathing mask connected her with Veda and *Questor*. Guided by the computers, she slowly made her way toward the position where the sub was supposed to be.

Visibility was so poor that she was almost on top of it before she realized she had reached her goal. Swimming alongside, she made her way toward the air lock.

Tristan swallowed against the dryness of his throat and glanced at his watch. He had barely three minutes of air left. Already he could feel the seeping lethargy of oxygen deprivation invading his body. His arms and legs felt heavy, the buzzing in both ears was much worse, and his vision was becoming blurred.

Were he to try to leave the sub in that condition, he knew he would not have a prayer of making the surface. Yet still he held on to hope. Cassia would come; he knew it. The only question was whether or not she would arrive in time.

Far off in the distance, he thought he heard a sound. At first, it seemed no more than a figment of his imagination. Then the sound was repeated more distinctly and he realized what he was hearing.

The air lock was opening. Drawing on the last of his strength, he forced himself to stand and make his way to the hatch. Elation surged through him as he watched the water gauge slowly empty. An instant later, the inner door flew open and a wet, disheveled Cassia stumbled into his arms.

"Tristan . . ." she gasped, wrenching off her mask. "Are you all right? I've been so worried . . ." The words trailed off as the full impact of the poisoned air struck her. Horror flashed across her face. Swiftly, she handed him the mask.

He filled his lungs long and gratefully, savoring the rush of life-giving oxygen. Then, as Cassia took her turn, he pulled on his flippers and mask. Together they stepped into the air lock.

Moments later they were free of the disabled sub. Tristan grasped her hand, and together they swam upward through the murky water, pausing every few minutes to share the single tank of oxygen.

Passing the mouthpiece back and forth was awkward and dangerous. Even the most experienced divers rigorously trained in rescue techniques hesitated to try it. But they had no difficulty. Their absolute trust in one another enabled them to share everything, including all that was necessary to sustain life.

They broke through to the surface, smiling broadly. Tristan had never seen a sight as lovely as the sky above him, unless it was the sight of Cassia's face transformed by love.

Together they reached the ship and pulled themselves on board. Even as they were doing so, the unnatural calm was ending. The eye of the storm was passing, and the full force of the hurricane was about to hit them again.

Chapter 18

QUESTOR RODE AT ANCHOR, TUCKED INTO A TINY harbor adjacent to a jewel-like island, one of the many uninhabited atolls clustered throughout the Caribbean.

Sheltered within the embracing arms of a pure white sand beach, and further protected by a barrier reef, the ship was safe from the pounding waves and howling winds that accompanied the second onslaught of the storm.

Cassia breathed a sigh of relief as the wild buffeting they had endured gave way to no more than a gentle rocking. They were safe, and they were together. She could ask for nothing more.

Tristan signed off on the radio and turned to her. His sea-green eyes gleamed as he said, "Sean has explained why he let you stay on board."

She raised a brow challengingly. "Oh, really? Didn't you believe me when I told you he had no choice?"

A broad grin slashed his burnished features. "That's his excuse, in a nutshell. He said you were just too much woman for him to handle." He moved toward her, his smile deepening. "I, on the other hand, feel more than capable."

The ripple of anticipation that darted through her made it very difficult to seem unconvinced, but she managed—barely. "Don't you think you should rest?"

Closing the distance between them, he shook his head. "Later." Stripped of all pretense, his gaze wandered over her ardently. In her simple maillot swimsuit, with her silvery hair plastered to her head and her skin slightly puckered from the chill of the storm, she was easily the most beautiful and desirable woman he had ever seen.

And she was his. Perhaps she didn't quite realize it yet, but she would. Very soon.

Bending, he lifted her easily in his arms and headed for the door. Taken by surprise, sort of, Cassia offered no protest. As naturally as though she had been there all her life, she settled against him and gave herself up to whatever he had in mind.

Her cabin was a warm, welcome haven after the turmoil of the storm. Tristan set her down gently, then disappeared into the bathroom, returning moments later with several towels.

"This is getting to be a habit," he murmured as he began to dry her.

"Hmmm . . . a very nice one."

"Don't get too comfortable. I have other things in mind."

Their eyes met, his darkly male, hers alight with the beginnings of tremulous joy. Trembling, she placed her hands on his broad chest. "Let me return the favor."

Tristan grew very still beneath her touch. His breathing was ragged, and a pulse beat in the corded column of his throat. But he allowed her full rein to do as she would.

With absolute concentration, Cassia unbuttoned his sodden shirt and slipped it from his wide shoulders, letting it drop onto the floor at their feet. A bit clumsily, but with growing confidence, she unsnapped his slacks and slid them down past his narrow hips and the steely length of his legs.

When only his briefs remained, she picked up a towel and began gently to dry his skin.

Tristan bore it as long as he could. The resurgence of life pounding through his veins made his self-control a precarious thing at best. He wanted her as he had never wanted anything, wanted to lose himself in her sweetness and at the same time take her with him to the heights of fulfillment.

Never a man to do anything by half measures, he was more than ready to fully and irrevocably commit himself to her. Cassia sensed the pressure building in him and, with the innate sensitivity of a woman in love, knew exactly when to stop her gentle torment.

The towel she had been using joined the other on the floor as she stepped a small distance away from him. He reached out to stop her, only to let his hands drop to his sides as he realized what she intended.

Their gazes were locked as, with artless grace, she removed her maillot and stood before him. Gravely, she said, "I love you, Tristan, and I would like very much to celebrate that."

His throat tightened painfully at the beauty of her, not merely of her body but of the spirit that flowed out to engulf him in the promise of womanly strength. A slight dampness misted his vision as he reached for her.

Huskily, he murmured, "I can't think of anything more worth rejoicing about, my love."

The smile that reached all the way to her eyes was radiant. The last of her doubts and her defenses had crumbled as though they had never been. Hand in hand, they walked to the bunk. Standing beside it, Tristan removed his briefs and drew her to him.

They embraced gently, with full awareness of the preciousness of life and how close they had come to losing it. That was enough, for a time. Then the embers of passion began to glow ever more brightly, and the urgent need to give expression to their love overcame them both.

Lying beneath him, Cassia delighted in the strength and power of his body, in the tenderness that poured from him with his every skillful touch and murmured word, and in her own ability to return touch for touch and word for word until they were engulfed in a storm of their own making.

Her body opened to him as fully as her heart and spirit. They were joined utterly, all pain washed away, all loneliness vanquished, the dream made reality.

Driving within her, Tristan found a welcome beyond anything he had ever known. She received him without restraint, yielding the citadel of her womanliness even as she took his seed within her, knowing somehow deep within her soul that this time it would become life.

Afterward, lying in the quiet haven of his arms, she laughed softly. "For two such intelligent people, it took us a while to figure this out."

He eyed her teasingly. "Oh, I knew all along. Why do you think I pursued you so relentlessly?"

She cast him a lovingly skeptical look. "Is that what you did? I thought you just asked me along for my technical expertise."

"That's what I told myself, until I found you with Hank right after we sailed. That poor guy! I was ready to kill him."

She nestled against him, not at all surprised to discover that she could recall that painful scene with fond nostalgia. Wonder shaded her voice as she said, "You were jealous?"

"Insanely. Of Hank . . . Sean . . . Jason." He shook his head ruefully. "Every one of my crew must be convinced by this time that I'm crazy. It's amazing that they stuck with me."

"Oh, there are compensations. You aren't so bad."

That earned her a very gentle slap on her bare bottom. "Witch. I still say you cast some sort of spell over me."

Through the thick fringes of her lashes she gave him a thoroughly feminine look. "What if I did? I don't see you struggling very hard."

He laughed wryly. "I'm not struggling at all. You see before you a willing captive. Now, what are you going to do about it?"

Cassia hesitated. She knew what she wanted to do, but wasn't quite sure that was what he meant. . . .

Tristan saw her doubt and was touched by it. How incredible that this woman who had given him the very key to his soul should lack confidence about his intentions.

Drawing her closer, their legs entwining, he murmured, "You wouldn't want to disappoint Veda and *Questor,* would you?"

She raised her head slightly, puzzled. "What do you mean?"

His mouth twitched and he announced, "They bought us a wedding present."

"A w-wedding present . . . ! How . . . ?"

"Simple. *Questor* hooked himself up to one of those computerized shopping services and they picked out something they thought we'd like."

"But how can they pay for it?"

"Oh, that's no problem. Veda beat the whole crew at poker the other night."

"Poker!"

He nodded somberly. "They made the mistake of

teaching her. Now she's got some idea about going to Vegas."

"Oh, no! That's where I draw the line. There's no way I'll let her get mixed up in anything like that!"

Laughing, Tristan rolled over, trapping her beneath him with loving fierceness. "Then, my sweet wife-to-be, I suggest we find some way to distract her. Before she leads *Questor* astray."

Rising passion made her voice quiver. "We'll go on with the excavation, of course."

Cupping a breast in his hand, he breathed gently against her. "Of course, but don't expect the world to accept what we've found immediately. Appesia and her tavern are going to stir up all sorts of controversy."

"I don't mind," she murmured, her hands twining in his hair. "Not as long as I've got you."

He raised his head slightly, the unabashed love in his gaze making her gasp softly. "You do, sweetheart. Forever."

Forever. A single word that was a vow. She returned it completely, knowing he was right. They had endured much to find each other. Now that the discovery was at last well and truly theirs, nothing would ever separate them.

Beyond the reaches of time and space, beyond the limits of physical life, so long as the human spirit could dare to dream, they would be together.

An epic novel of exotic rituals
and the lure of the Upper Amazon

THE TAKERS RIVER OF GOLD

JERRY AND S.A. AHERN

THE TAKERS are the intrepid Josh Culhane and the seductive Mary Mulrooney. These two adventurers launch an incredible journey into the Brazilian rain forest. Far upriver, the jungle yields its deepest secret—the lost city of the Amazon warrior women!

THE TAKERS series is making publishing history. Awarded *The Romantic Times* first prize for High Adventure in 1984, the opening book in the series was hailed by *The Romantic Times* as "the next trend in romance writing and reading. Highly recommended!"

Jerry and S.A. Ahern have never been better!